I'VE COME TO TALK WITH YOU AGAIN

*A collection of short stories inspired by the songs
I grew up loving*

Leo Jahn

NORSTRILIA PRESS

NORSTRILIA PRESS

11 Robe Street, St Kilda 3182 Australia

norstriliapress.com

Cover design by Fantoons.

Book design by David Grigg

Typeset in Charter and Barlow

ISBN 978-1-7638516-2-7 (paperback)

ISBN 978-1-7638516-3-4 (eBook)

I'VE COME TO TALK WITH YOU AGAIN

Ten short stories inspired by songs that ingrained
themselves in Leo Jahn's brain when he first
listened to AM radio as a teenager. Some relate to
personal experiences while others provide back
stories to the characters in the songs.
This is a unique and moving collection of
surprising short stories.

*"A fascinating collection … that unveils a new and
exciting experience through each piece."*

— Kim Robyn Smith

*"A wonderfully original collection of stories that reflects
a profound love of music. Leo Jahn shows us worlds where
opportunities must be taken, where there is success for
those willing to work for it, and sometimes tragedy for the
less fortunate. Written in a distinctive lyrical style these
are realistic stories about life lessons and the value of
compassion and love. Their broad scope and meaning
highlight the importance of listening to music for
inspiration throughout life."*

— Prue Mercer

CONTENTS

Preface   1

Hush Little Baby   5

All The Lonely People   25

I've Come to Talk with You Again   37

Starry Night   65

It's Gonna Be A Long, Long Time   83

You've Got Us Feeling Alright   109

Colitas in the Desert   123

The Pledge   141

Those Days Are Over   171

Way on Down South   193

To Silvia,

my wife and companion of four decades. My rock, the one who has endured life by my side—thank you for your patience, your love, and for pretending to be interested every time I said, "I have an idea for my next story."

To my brilliant children, Sylvia H. and Gustavo.

You are the reason and the inspiration behind everything I do. Thanks for mastering the art of pretending to listen to my story ideas.

And to Juan Carlos,

my loyal reader, oldest friend, and the only person who's read *everything* I've written—*in two languages*, no less. Either you're incredibly supportive or incredibly bored.

Over fifty years of friendship, separated by thousands of kilometres, yet every time we meet, it's like no time has passed—just two old guys, a cold beer, and the same tired jokes about Canadians and Australians (he still insists maple syrup is a food group).

Special mention to my friends of the Sandringham Library's Writing Group, who helped me in tightening up these stories.

Thanks to all of you—without your love, humour, and occasional eye-rolls, this collection wouldn't exist. Or worse, it might be longer.

Preface

Even though I'm not a musician there has always been music in my life.

I remember the long road trips with the family, back in my native Venezuela, where my dad used to play traditional music from our country on the car's cassette player. The tunes by Aldemaro Romero and Gualberto Ibarreto filled the air and the five of us sang the songs we had heard dozens of times before.

My mum always had the radio on when driving us to school, and we listened to the hits of the moment. I tried to memorize the lyrics, mostly by making up the words, as I didn't speak English back then.

When in my room, I always had the radio on and sometimes I called the DJs to make requests. You have to remember that there was no digital music and no streaming back then. Access to money to buy records was limited when I was twelve, so the best chance of listening to my favourite songs was to be glued to the radio waiting for them to be played. I remember how happy I felt when one of my songs was finally aired. I had limited visual information about the bands therefore my teenage brain created images of what I thought Santana, Donna Summer and The Eagles looked like.

Some of these songs, heard firstly and mainly on scratchy AM radio stations, became ingrained in my brain. Songs which I didn't understand at first due to the language barrier, but which I loved for the music itself.

As I grew older, and older, and older, my musical taste expanded and evolved, and thanks to the magic of streaming services I'm always listening to new trends and artists. I have also discovered bands, originated in the sixties and seventies, which were not as popular back then but created superb music.

But amidst this evolution and expansion of my musical library, one thing has remained constant, and this is my love for those songs I listened to on my small radio, sometimes late at night when my brother was already sound asleep.

These songs played a part in my coming of age as a young adult, and all of them have a particular significance for me. This collection contains ten stories inspired by songs from this part of my life when I was growing up and deciding who I wanted to be.

There are stories here which relate to personal experiences while others are inspired by my interpretation of the lyrics. In other cases, I just wanted to provide the back stories to the characters which form part of the song. Most of the songs are pop-rock hits, although I slipped in a jazz standard which I have loved from the first time I heard Ella Fitzgerald when I was twelve.

After everything has been said and done, and regardless of the success (or lack of) of this collection, this is my humble tribute to ten songs which helped me grow into the man I am now and will always form part of my favourites playlist.

I hope you enjoy reading them.

Hush Little Baby

After George and Ira Gershwin

1918

"C'mon Mia, dinner is served. You don't want the food to go cold."

Mia did not move. She had been looking through the window for a long time. A couple of hours maybe? Her gaze was fixated on the bright orange ball on the horizon which was slowly being swallowed by the waters of the Ocmulgee.

"What are we gonna do, Mrs. Delaney? That child ain't eating anymore."

"Don't you worry, Louise. Leave her plate on the table and cover it. She'll eventually eat."

Louise did as she was told. Louise always did as she was told. If there was something in life that Louise was good at, it was doing what she was told to do.

The large black woman covered the porcelain plate which contained fried chicken, potatoes and greens. A dim cloud of steam puffed out of the dish when a second plate was used to cover the meal.

Before retiring to her quarters, Louise prepared a chamomile tea with honey for Mrs. Delaney, which she had every night after supper.

"Thanks, Louise. You're a gem."

Even though Mrs. Delaney said these words to her maid frequently, it always made Louise blush a little. The compliments from her boss came hand in hand with an honest smile, a smile that started in her deep green eyes and was enhanced by every crease and wrinkle on her face. Mrs. Delaney was a good woman.

Louise gave Mia one last look. She had not moved an inch from her position at the windowsill. The sun had already disappeared although beams of a dying orange light were still tinting the clouds in the horizon. No sign of the grackles. No sign of Jerome.

1909

"Take the girl inside, the negroes are returning from the fields!"

The instructions from Brock Delaney made Louise jump from her chair in the kitchen, where she had been busy preparing supper.

"C'mon Mia, time to go to your room. You need to have a bath before dinner."

"Why does my father make you hide me from the cotton pickers? You're a negro too," said Mia.

"I don't know, my child. I'm just an ignorant maid following orders, that's all."

"But you love me, don't you? Negroes can love too, I think."

"Of course, I love you, Mia, you don't need to ask me this every day," said Louise, while closing the girl's bedroom door behind them.

"Then why aren't the cotton pickers allowed to see me?"

"Because they are men, and black men cannot mingle with little white ladies like you," Louise was hoping Mia would stop asking questions.

"Does this mean that when I grow older, like fifteen, and I'm not a little white lady anymore, they will be allowed to see me?"

"Oh God, when will she stop," thought Louise.

"Yes, my dear, eventually you will be allowed to see the negroes and they will be allowed to see you too. You will even bring them food and drink to their quarters, like your Ma does now."

"Will Jerome be a cotton picker too? I don't want him to become one, or my father won't let me see him anymore."

Louise smiled at Mia, who looked at her with the same penetrating green eyes her mother had, and a small round face framed with light brown wavy hair.

"I don't know, my child. He's still too young."

Jerome was only eleven, just a year older than Mia, and in one year he would be working in the cotton fields with the rest of the men. Louise knew what this meant but didn't have the heart to tell the truth to her beloved Mia.

At least not now.

⌒

"Look Mia. I caught this one for you." The red bird the boy was holding in his hands was fiercely flapping its wings trying to escape.

"You caught a cardinal. He's beautiful!"

The children stared at the bright plumage of the scared bird, and realised they could not keep it. They knew each other so well that they almost read the other's mind. Mia and Jerome looked at each other, and without saying another word, Jerome released the bird, which flew away as fast as its wings allowed it to.

"Do you know I can tell when you're coming to the big house to visit?" said Mia.

"How can you do that?"

"Because of the grackles. They nest on top of the oak trees along the main road, and they are easily startled. Whenever someone is coming, they leave their nests and start squeaking and croaking. Then I know there's someone coming. I always hope it's you."

Jerome smiled.

"Let's go fishing. I have my net and rod by the bridge."

"I'll go if you promise me you'll release the fishes. And no hooks, use only the net."

The first time Mia went fishing with Jerome, and he caught a large redeye, she stared in horror at the hook which had pierced the fishes' mouth. Jerome went from being a proud fisherman to an apologetic friend in seconds, and promised her he would never hurt a fish again.

The children sat on the rocks near the bridge and dipped their toes in the coppery water. Mia didn't like the feeling of her feet against the slimy riverbed, but Jerome didn't care. He never used shoes anyway. He walked a couple of meters into the river, with water almost by his waist, and dipped the fishing net.

"Hey, here's the first one. What is it? What is it?"

"It's a shiner, surely it is!" replied the girl. Jerome put the small fish into a bucket with water.

After a while, a larger fish got caught in Jerome's net.

"That's a largemouth, surely it is! Don't put it in the

bucket or he'll eat the poor shiner." Mia enjoyed that game.

The boy released the largemouth bass back into the river.

Jerome kept catching fish and Mia showing her knowledge of Georgia's freshwater species, something she learned from her father.

The squeaking of grackles, followed by the clatter of hooves hitting the dirt road, announced that Brock Delaney was approaching the house. Jerome stared at Mia. Mister Delaney scared him.

"Don't worry, Jerome. My father likes you. He told me so."

"But I will be a cotton picker soon. And your father doesn't like you near cotton pickers."

"You're a child still. Look at you, skinnier than me. How can my father be worried about you?"

The imposing figure of Brock Delaney, mounting his mighty horse Cerberus, stood next to the children. A desperate catfish was fighting for freedom in Jerome's net. The boy's eyes were fixated on the boss.

"Release that catfish now boy, or it's gonna die soon," commanded Delaney in his deep and raspy voice.

Jerome slowly returned the net to the water and helped the fish back out to the river.

"Mia, come with me, we need to go back to the house. I don't want you out here alone with this boy."

"But dad, we were only fishing. I was calling all the

species correctly and Jerome was releasing them all back. I enjoy that game."

"I wasn't asking. Just come here now. And you, boy, go back to the barracks. Your mother must be worried sick."

And that was that.

From that day onwards, Mia was only allowed to see Jerome when in the company of her parents or Louise, and strictly during festivities or at the Church on Sundays.

They did, however, find ways of meeting in secret whenever they could, making sure to avoid Louise's constant supervision of Mia.

1913

"Remember how we used to fish by the bridge, and I called all the species by their names?"

"Yeah, until your father told us not to see each other."

"But we haven't exactly been following his orders, have we?"

Mia was always the more adventurous of the two. Living a privileged life gave her the chance of being courageous and daring. Nothing could harm her. Especially in the summertime, when the living was easy.

On the other hand, Jerome was now, at sixteen, a grown man, and had to work in the cotton fields to earn his meals and a roof above his head. There were no adventures for Jerome to follow. The only things he could follow were the orders of the foreman or Mister Delaney, and pray that he wouldn't get whipped.

Mia took Jerome's hand.

Her little white fingers were swallowed by Jerome's. He was a big boy. They looked at each other and Jerome planted a kiss on her lips. It lasted a couple of seconds and Jerome pulled away, scared of what could happen if someone saw them.

"That felt great, Jerome. I've never kissed anyone before," said Mia, still holding his hand.

"It was my first time too. I've never felt anything like this before."

Mia kissed him again, and this time it became more passionate. For Mia, this was the love story she had been dreaming of for the past two years.

For Jerome, there were mixed feelings. On the one hand he loved Mia, and had always felt that way, but he knew there were boundaries he should never cross if he wanted to survive, and this was one of them. He could hear his mother saying *"Don't mess with white girls, boy. Stick to your kind,"* and he was not only messing with a white girl, but the daughter of his employer.

"We can't do this. Your father would kill me if he found out,"

"Nonsense. I will tell him we love each other."

"Are you crazy? Don't ever tell him that. There is no place for me in your life. We need to call this off now, or I could be facing a whip to my backside."

"You're stupid and a coward. You should learn to stand up for yourself. I'm going now. Whenever you decide to man up, come and fetch me." Mia ran back to the house, sobbing.

Jerome's words forced Mia to take a glimpse inside real life. She had been living in a fantasy world where everything she wanted was served on a silver platter. Everything but the love of a black cotton picker working for her father.

That night, Mia sat by the window, watching the sunset, and weeping quietly. Louise brought her an iced tea and stared at the horizon. She knew what the problem was and put her arms around Mia's tiny body without asking her anything.

"You see, my girl, this is summer, the best time of the year in Georgia. Look out there, the sun is shining, fish are jumping in the Ocmulgee and the cotton is ready for picking. You have rich dad and a beautiful and kind mom. So, hush little baby, don't cry no more."

Mia smiled and kissed Louise on the cheek. Whenever there was trouble, Louise was there to remind her how good a life she had, and that there was always hope of a better future.

But today, she had stepped into the world where most people lived, and she didn't like what she saw.

Her heart had been broken.

1917

"So, when is it that you're leaving for Atlanta?"

The girl stared absently at the horizon. She had agreed to meet with Julien, the son of a banker who was friends with her father, just out of courtesy, but she couldn't wait for the visit to be over.

"Sorry, what? Ah, Atlanta. Yes, I haven't made up my mind yet. My father wants me to go to college, but I'm not sure this is what I want."

They were sitting on the front porch of the big house, with a magnificent view of the Ocmulgee. Louise had left a tray with lemonade and biscuits for them.

Julien took Mia's hand, and she immediately reacted by pulling away. She did this in the polite way expected from a Southern lady, but with enough firmness to let him know she was not interested.

"Sorry, Mia. Apologies if this was too bold of me."

"Nonsense, Julian. Don't give this too much thought. It's just that I'm not interested in you that way. Let's go back with our parents in the backyard."

Louise frowned from her vantage point in the living room, where she was sent to spy on Mia and her interaction with this potential suitor. *"Another rejection. That girl is surely stubborn,"* she thought.

For the past two years, the Delaneys had been searching for a good man to marry their daughter. A bunch of men, handpicked by Brock or Helen Delaney, had been invited to the house. Given the number of boys Mia had turned away, the next strategy was to send her to the University of Georgia in Atlanta. Mia was not too interested in this either. She told her parents she'd rather stay in the farm and work in the family business.

"Louise, you spend a lot of time with Mia. She confides in you, I'm sure. And I know you always want the best for her. Tell me please, has she been seeing Jerome behind our backs?"

"If she has, she hasn't told me. I have always asked her to stay away from Jerome because you're right, them kids being together means nothing but trouble."

Louise wasn't being totally honest with Mrs. Delaney, but she wasn't lying either. Mia *had* secretly been seeing Jerome. Twice a week, after sunset, Jerome walked from the barracks to the big house, and Mia climbed out of her bedroom window to greet him at the bridge. Louise could tell by listening to the grackles squeaking, startled by the young man's presence. Every Tuesday and Friday. Same time. Mia never told Louise anything, which gave the black woman the gift of anonymity.

In God's eyes, she wasn't lying to Mrs. Delaney.

"Every time I come here to meet you, I think your father is going to appear out of nowhere with his 12 gauge."

"Don't be dramatic, Jerome. After supper he drinks

two glasses of brandy and falls asleep immediately. There is no chance of us getting caught."

"What about Louise? That woman is practically your mom's personal spy. Don't you fear she will find out?"

"She won't tell my mom before letting me know first, and I'll convince her to keep her mouth shut. She is terrified of my father finding out and what that could mean for us."

"You mean, what it would mean for me. He will probably lock you in your room for weeks, but I will be whipped and thrown in jail, if not killed by a bullet to my head."

"That's nonsense. Have you ever seen my father whip anyone, much less shoot anyone? Never, right? He can be a hard boss, but he's not cruel."

Jerome wanted to say he had indeed seen Brock Delaney whip one of the cotton pickers, but that was for raping a coloured girl. He chose to keep this to himself. Besides, Brock had taught Jerome to read and write. He was actually the only man in the barracks capable of doing so.

The pair kissed and cuddled for a while. Their encounters didn't involve sex. Mia wanted to save this for when they got married. Jerome knew the chances of this ever happening were slim.

"You know this war in Europe, maybe it's a sign that the world is changing. I hope that when the war is over, there will be more understanding between all people and the barriers that divide us disappear. What do you think?"

"I think you may be right. This is why I enlisted in the Army. I'm supposed to be leaving for Atlanta on Sunday."

There, he said it. He had been holding on to this secret for weeks and had finally found the moment to tell her.

"But ... are blacks even allowed to enlist? I thought they were not, and I had never heard of a coloured recruit."

"Not by the Navy, but the Army is accepting black recruits. I just want to serve my country and fight for a better world for us."

Mia was stunned by the news. She wanted to feel happy for Jerome, but she feared for his life. The accounts of young men dying in the war or returning from Europe without an arm or a leg were horrifying.

"I don't know what to say. I'm proud but scared to lose you at the same time. Please promise you will be careful and write to me every day." Mia's voice broke when she said these words.

That was the last time Jerome and Mia saw each other before he took the train to Atlanta.

1918

"Any news from the war?" said Helen to her husband Brock who had just arrived from Juliette.

"There is a massive attack by the Allies on the Western Front. According to the paper, this is the biggest offensive in the United States' military history. I believe Wilson wants to end the war now."

"And no letter from Jerome?" asked Mia.

"Sorry, Mia. No letter from him."

Brock, Helen, and Louise watched as Mia slumped onto the couch by the windowsill. This had been her preferred spot in the house from the time she stopped receiving letters from Jerome, more than three months ago. The Army wasn't sure of his location, and with the chaos in Europe, thousands of families in the United States were completely unaware of the whereabouts of their relatives.

These were cruel times.

Since Jerome left Juliette, he had constantly written to Mia. Even from the days in the training facility in Savannah. The letters were picked up by Brock at the Juliette Post Office. At first, Brock opened the letters and read them before giving them to Mia. But Brock was surprised by how polite the young man was when addressing his daughter, and moved by the love he had for her.

It was Brock who convinced Jerome to join the Army,

in part because Brock thought highly of the young man, but also to keep him away from Mia. He was now as worried for his wellbeing as the rest of the family were.

Brock was now going to Juliette every day to find out about the war, and hoping for a letter from Jerome. The offensive at the Meuse-Argonne front was all the papers wrote about, and the end of the war seemed imminent.

One day in October, Brock picked up a letter from the post. Not from Jerome, but from the US Army. The letter was addressed to Mia. Brock didn't dare to open it, in fear of what it might say.

When he arrived at the house, he gave the envelope to Mia, who opened it with trembling fingers.

"Dear Miss Delaney,

We hope this letter finds you well.

We regret to say that during the Battle of the Meuse-Argonne there have been many casualties, and even though we have not found his body or corresponding identity tag, we cannot account for the whereabouts of Mr. Jerome Walker and presume he has gallantly died in combat.

Our condolences to yourself and Corporal Walker's family and may he rest in peace.

Yours faithfully,
General Robert E. Coombs"

"I'm sorry baby, this must be very hard for you," said Helen to her daughter, who was still going over the letter.

"They haven't found his body. He may still be alive, Mom." Mia sobbed and covered her face with her arms, trying to hang on to the faintest glimpse of hope possible.

Brock embraced his daughter, who was now crying unconsolably. Louise and Helen were also crying, not only feeling sad for Mia, but because, now that he was absent, they had grown to care about Jerome by reading his letters to Mia.

Louise sat down with Mia in the sofa by the window, watching the sunset. It was a clear autumn afternoon. Mia was sobbing silently.

"I know you're hurting but believe me when I say this will pass. One of these mornings, you're gonna wake up singing. But till that mornin' there's nothing can harm you, with mom and dad standing by."

Mia looked at Louise and flashed a smile. She loved that woman and the simple way she had of seeing the world. But maybe this is how things should be for her. Simple and uncomplicated.

"You're unique, Louise. Do you know that? Don't you ever dare to leave me as well."

"I'll never leave you, my child. You can count on that."

The days passed, and finally in November the Germans surrendered to the Allies, ending the most devastating war known to humankind. For the next few weeks, American survivors arrived back to their homes and families. Some of them healthy, but many of them with life changing injuries.

One afternoon in December, just before Christmas, Helen and Louise were sitting on the front porch with Mia. It was a Sunday, and the cotton workers were gathered in their barracks, resting before the start of another week of hard work.

The three women were drinking lemonade, when a familiar sound could be heard over the oak trees.

"Do you hear that?" asked Mia.

"What? The birds?" replied Helen.

"Not any birds Mrs. Delaney. These are grackles. Something has startled them," said Louise.

"On a Sunday? Who could be arriving here on a Sunday?" said Helen and turned to look at Mia, but the girl was already running towards the bridge.

All The Lonely People

After Paul McCartney

As soon as the bride and groom left St. Peter's in their black Rolls Royce, Eleanor started collecting rice grains from the stone steps with her little broom and bucket, much to the surprise of the crowd who gathered at the Church's gate.

Father McCarthy stared at the woman he knew very well. As opposed to the wedding attendees, he was used to seeing her weaving on her knees between legs and heels trying to fill her tin bucket. She was also the most fervent churchgoer in the parish, never missing the three weekly services.

A few seconds after the priest turned around to greet a smiling young couple, he heard a clank and someone calling for help.

"Somebody help me please!" said a middle-aged man in a dark suit, "I think I hit this lady on the head!"

Eleanor lay flat on her back, her right hand on her forehead, while the man took his jacket off, folded it into a pillow and put it behind her head. Another woman was waving her hands in front of Eleanor's face giving her some air. The tin bucket was upside down, its meagre contents spread unevenly on the marble floor.

"Oh Eleanor, Eleanor. How are you feeling, darling?" said Father McCarthy, kneeling besides her.

"I'm okay father, nothing to worry about. I need to be more careful. This wasn't his fault. I was just crawling too low and he didn't see me." Eleanor flashed a smile to the priest and both men helped her sit up.

"I'm really sorry, Miss," said her inadvertent attacker. "I hope I didn't hurt you too badly."

"Nothing to worry about, love. I'm just getting clumsier with age, that's all. But carry on, please, don't mind me. If you could please help me pick up my rice I'll be out of here in a jiffy." Within seconds a young boy of about twelve had brushed the small amount of rice back into the bucket and presented it to the old lady, who grabbed it with the emotion of an athlete picking up a trophy.

"Do you want some water, Eleanor? You can also rest here with me until you feel well," said the priest.

"Thanks, Father. You're always so kind to me but I'm perfectly all right and need to get home to feed my boys. See you on Sunday."

The elderly woman walked away from the Church at the pace her short legs allowed. She was wearing one of her usual flowery dresses, mostly pink and yellow with matching pink shoes, handbag and lipstick. Her short auburn hair remained perfectly still, even after the unfortunate knee to the head. Her neck was adorned with a triple pearl necklace that matched her earrings. She always reminded the priest of his favourite auntie, the one who slipped a ten-pound note in his hand when he visited her on Sundays in his youth.

Father McCarthy waited until the rest of the wedding attendees left and closed the heavy Church gates behind him, hoping Eleanor would make it to her house without further trouble.

Eleanor emptied the contents of the bucket in a jar which once contained raspberry conserve. The jar was now half full. A few more weddings and she would be able to cook a full cup.

"Oh, come on boys, you're getting too spoiled. It's not even time for your supper yet," she said to her two Siamese cats, who purred and meowed while rubbing against her legs. She filled their bowls with cat food and replenished their water containers. Eleanor then opened her fridge to see what she could have for dinner. A couple of tomatoes stared at her like big red eyes from the top shelf. She picked them only to realise they were sitting in a pool of their own juice, the skin wrinkly and the meat soft. She tossed them in the rubbish bin which was already full to the brim. She scoured behind sauce bottles and milk cartons for any leftovers but couldn't find anything to eat.

"I'm not hungry anyway," she mumbled to herself while closing the fridge door.

She looked out the window and saw the unmistakable tall and lean figure of her husband arriving home from work. Her face brightened and she went for the front door to greet him. Eleanor walked down the five steps separating her front porch from the concrete path leading to the picket fence, but George wasn't there anymore.

The rusty hinges creaked as she opened the gate at the fence. Eleanor looked left and right. The identical front yards of the identical suburban houses lining both sides of Cochrane Street were devoid of any human life. The only sign of life in her surroundings came from the wagging tail of a Golden Retriever behind the fence of the house opposite hers. At first, she thought George could have wandered off to the shops to fetch some smokes, but reality started sinking in. She felt both sad and ashamed, a terrible combination of feelings, and slowly walked back to the house.

She stepped into the living room and turned on the TV to watch the news. She sat on the worn-out sofa whose filling had morphed through the years adapting to her body like a giant glove. The news unfolded in front of her: a Member of Parliament had resigned due to an alleged sex scandal; the Queen was attending some sort of celebration at Westminster Cathedral; the Prime Minister met with the United States' Secretary of State. When the sports segment started she stood up to change channels. A couple of turns of the dial and she landed into a documentary about the war which immediately summoned memories of George.

She turned to see the framed photo of her husband in his Army uniform hanging from the wall. He was a tall, thin and handsome man. Her beloved George, a fighter pilot for the Royal Air Force who went missing in action during the Berlin bombings and whose body was never recovered. Fifteen years after the war ended a fat man with pink cheeks who barely fit in his uniform knocked on her door one night. He told her he was flying next to George and saw him crash into the Berlin Parliament in his Spitfire. Only then did she manage to accept his death. Only then she did stop sending letters to the Air Force demanding an account of her husband's whereabouts. A symbolic funeral was held at St. Peter's Church with a memorable sermon by Father McCarthy who spoke beautifully about George, making it look as if he had known him for years.

On a shelf underneath the photo, she kept the Victoria Cross medal awarded to him posthumously. She never quite made up her mind about this medal. It was supposed to be a high honour but for her this piece of metal attached to a string was the polite way the British Government apologised to Eleanor for sending her husband to his death.

Eleanor opened the bottle of brandy she had started recently. Was it the day before? It was still half full. She poured a serving in a glass and drank it all in one continuous sip. A wave of warmth filled her insides and opened her nostrils. She took the bottle and glass back to the sofa where she plunged, causing some of the liquid to spill out, the amber drops quickly blending with the fabric of the sofa and magically disappearing. She continued to drink while watching the documentary with disinterest and crying in silence.

That night she went to sleep once again without anything in her stomach but alcohol, or anything in her heart but pain.

⌇

Fergus McCarthy washed his socks and hung them to dry on the clothesline that ran from one wall to the other in his kitchen. He had two pairs of woollen socks and washed them once a week. He didn't mind the smell of sweaty old socks as long as it came from his own feet. He filled the stove to the max hoping the socks would dry quicker this way. This usually worked but during the wetter months he sometimes had to put on wet socks the next day.

"Ah, Fergus, you're getting fucking old, mate," he said to the person in the mirror, the man with sagging boobs, sagging chin and sagging flesh under his arms. The portion of his head which had grown past his silver hair was shiny and had dark spots scattered along the surface. Yes, there was no doubt that Fergus McCarthy, once a young heartthrob who roamed the streets of Galway drinking scotch with his mates, was now an old man.

Father McCarthy liked to call himself Fergus when alone in his miniature apartment at the back of St. Peters. He enjoyed fantasizing about what could have been had he chosen a different career path. He thought of himself as a professional football player in England's First Division. A defender for Liverpool perhaps. Being a famous personality, he would meet movie stars like Elizabeth Taylor or Grace Kelly and maybe even date them. Well, not Grace Kelly. She was married to that prince anyway. But Elizabeth Taylor was different. Maybe he could have charmed her while she roamed through European cities when in between husbands. Maybe. He had a poster of Taylor pinned to the wall just opposite where the thick cross with the somewhat beefed-up Jesus Christ hung.

Fergus wasn't ashamed of his fantasies about women. He used to say to himself *"Just because I'm on a diet it doesn't mean I can't enjoy reading the menu."* At the end of the day, he had never broken his chastity vows in the thirty years since he was ordained. Even though he continuously questioned his calling and said to himself *"what if"* as his mind wandered through the options he never explored and the chances he didn't take, he always came back down to reality and decided he would make the same decision again if he had the opportunity. At least that's what he liked telling himself.

Dressed only in his underwear, he sat down under his dripping socks, took a sip of whiskey, scratched his balls and opened the Bible. He was now ready to write the sermon for the next Sunday service.

A sermon very few people would listen to and even fewer would care about.

⌒〜⌒

"Now brothers and sisters, I want to remind you of the gospel I preached to you," said Father McCarthy from the pulpit to the couple of dozen people scattered across the church. All eyes were on him, but he wasn't sure how many ears were listening.

"By this gospel you are saved, if you hold firmly to the word I preach to you. Otherwise, you have believed in vain." An anonymous cough echoed in the air. The priest didn't take long to find Eleanor's eyes firmly looking at him from her usual spot in the front pew.

He continued to read the sermon he had written based on a chapter in the New Testament about the Resurrection of Christ. He heard his own baritone voice projecting across the place with the aid of a microphone and speakers and the perfect acoustics of an 18th Century church.

Minutes into his sermon and he saw how people started to lose interest. Some of them looked at their watches, others whispered in their partner's ears, a few more started to drowse. But not Eleanor. She was sitting still with her lips curled into a half smile and not taking her eyes off the priest. Father McCarthy could swear she didn't blink during his sermons.

When the sermon was over the organist played the first chords of a hymn. The public started to mumble the lyrics but the high pitched and out of tune voice of Eleanor quickly rose over the crowd and found its way into Father McCarthy's eardrums. Her face contorted as she sang like she was in a trance. Still no blinking.

At the end of the service, Father McCarthy stood outside the gates greeting the parishioners as they left the church with their souls cleansed and fresh for another week of sinning.

As soon as the churchgoers dispersed, the priest closed the heavy gates and walked to the back of the church, switching lights off and blowing candles as he went by.

"Eleanor?" said Father McCarthy when he saw her still sitting in her preferred pew.

The woman didn't answer or move.

When Father McCarthy reached Eleanor, he immediately knew he was staring at a dead body. He couldn't detect a breath or pulse, but it was more than that. She had become too skinny, there were bags under her eyes and her body reeked of alcohol and filth.

He felt guilty. He had visited Eleanor through the years when he felt she needed some personal support but stopped a year or so ago. Spending an afternoon at a smelly and badly kept house listening to Eleanor talking about her husband was not exactly appealing. But when he became a priest, he didn't sign up for appealing, he did it to help others, and he had failed this poor woman at a time she needed him the most.

⁓

The day of the funeral was cold and gloomy. The light drizzle and dark skies foreshadowed worse weather was on its way. Father McCarthy thought it seemed appropriate that a miserable life like Eleanor's ended in a miserable day like this.

He delayed the ceremony for a few minutes waiting to see if anyone else showed up but it soon became evident that the five people around the grave would be the only ones in attendance. One of them was Luigi, the Italian grocer who was there with his wife. Both were wearing strict black outfits as good Italians usually do. They went to the funerals of every one of their customers. There were two other widows who were nearly as devout as Eleanor. It looked like becoming a heartfelt Catholic was directly related to losing a spouse. The last of the attendants was Colin Scott, a stocky bald man wearing an expensive dark suit who was Eleanor's solicitor and executor of her estate. There were no family members.

"We are gathered here to celebrate the life of Eleanor and to pray for her soul. At this very moment she would be reunited with George, her husband and only man in her life. We all know how much Eleanor suffered after George was killed in the War during the Berlin raids."

"Dear Eleanor, you will be dearly remembered by all of those whose lives you touched. You were a kind person who never caused anyone harm. You frequently contributed to St. Peter's events and charities and were an enthusiastic participant at the Sunday services. We will all remember you with love. May God have mercy on your soul."

The ceremony continued and after a few more prayers, the cheap coffin, donated by the church as they did with their poorest parishioners, was lowered to its final position. The drizzle turned into rain forcing the miniature crowd to disperse and final formalities were forgotten.

Father McCarthy rubbed his hands, something he did after every funeral, like shaking death away from him. As much as he believed in salvation, and as pointless as his life was, he loved every minute of his time on this earth.

Before leaving he read the tombstone, which he had ordered:

HERE RESTS ELEANOR WHITBY.

LOVING WIFE OF GEORGE WHITBY.

YOU WILL BE DEARLY REMEMBERED.

1902-1963

I've Come to Talk with You Again

After Paul Simon

June 1964 – Brooklyn, New York

TODAY IS THE DAY YOU WILL BE SAVED MY FRIEND.

Jonas read the graffiti and smiled. He was sure the subway prophet had written this for him once again.

The screeching sound of a train entering the station made him realise he needed to run to the platform.

He couldn't miss this train.

Not today.

He sat at the end carriage, which would leave him closest to the Maple Street exit. Jonas quickly scanned his surroundings, but when the gates closed no one else had joined him. He was lucky, as most people taking the train from the Church Avenue Station at 7 a.m. on a Saturday were either junkies or criminals. Jonas clutched the gym bag against his chest and closed his eyes, dozing off to the clickety clack of the train as it sped north.

"Blessed is he who, in the name of charity and good will, shepherds the weak through the valley of the darkness, for he is truly his brother's keeper and the finder of lost children."

Jonas opened his eyes and saw a large black man, holding a book against his chest. A Bible, probably.

"Not a preacher. Not at seven in the morning, please," Jonas thought as he straightened in his seat. He felt the switchblade in his pocket. Preachers and muggers were interchangeable in the depths of the tunnels.

"And I will strike down upon thee with great vengeance and furious anger those who attempt to poison and destroy my brothers. And you will know I am the Lord when I lay My vengeance upon you."

The preacher pointed directly at Jonas when he finished his sentence and stared at him as if waiting for some response.

"Why me?" thought Jonas, when realising there were at least ten other passengers in the car. "Hey, buddy, would you let this brother rest for a bit?" he said. "I have a busy day ahead and need this half an hour to sleep."

"Oh, you're one of those. I know your type, my friend. Only thinking about how much money you can make, and the many things you can do with that money. You know how I call your type? Materialistic pigs!" said the preacher opening his arms and looking at the heavens, or in this case the graffitied ceiling of the train.

"You're right on the money, Father, a materialistic pig I am. Would you then give me a blessing to see if I change my ways?" replied Jonas.

Noticing the sarcasm, the man approached Jonas. His eyes seemed to be darting in all directions, and he was drenched in sweat. This was one zonked preacher.

"Hey, buddy," Jonas said. "Stop it right there. If you don't want to give me a blessing, that's fine, but leave me the fuck alone, will you?"

The preacher started making boxing moves with his hands. He was in his fifties and had a decent sized torso, but surely he was slow.

"Here we go," said Jonas as he stood up, leaving the bag on the seat. He took his hoodie off revealing a t-shirt which tightly wrapped his upper body, enhancing his bulging and well-groomed muscles. He also took a boxer's stance, waiting for his opponent's first move.

"Oh, the pig wants to play. Okay big boy. Show me what you got."

"Listen, old man, I don't want to hurt you, but if you get any closer, you will be missing a few teeth when you leave this train."

"I know a thing or two about fighting, boy. When you were sucking from your mama's tits I was already killing Nazis in France, so I got you covered."

There were laughs from the other passengers, who were keen to see some on board entertainment.

The preacher threw a right hand straight to his opponent's face. As Jonas expected, this was done almost in slow motion, although the preacher surely thought he was fast as lighting. Jonas took a step back, clear of the strike, and replied with a right hook to the liver which made the man twist in pain.

Not giving him chance to recover, Jonas threw his left hand right to the man's face, crushing his nose and making him fall on his back, blood spraying onto the side walls of the car.

The small crowd cheered in delight. Good show for a Saturday morning.

"Next time try picking on someone your own age, old man."

Jonas handed the whimpering preacher a handker-chief.

He got off the train at the next station and walked the two blocks to the gym. Now that he had warmed up his arms, getting his legs in shape before the workout seemed like a good idea.

"If only tonight's fight would be that easy," he thought.

July 1956 - Alvin, Texas

"This is the third time this year, Jonas, the third time!" Mary Jo was angry, and when she was angry her driving became more erratic. More than usual. The battered Buick, a car which the locals feared when they saw it speeding down the road, was swerving from side to side.

"Mama, I told you, they were making fun of Dad and calling you names. I won't stop fighting unless they leave me alone," replied Jonas from the back seat.

"O shit!" screamed Mary Jo when she realised she had gone through a red light and almost got t-boned by a Cadillac. She pulled over and waited for her heartbeat to return to normal. Jonas reached out over the set and hugged his mum, who quietly sobbed in the arms of her fourteen-year-old son.

"It's okay, Mama. Mister Giles knows these boys are trying to bully me all the time. He just followed procedure by calling you and sending me home. I bet you that Billy got a good ass kicking from him in front of his mum."

Mary Jo reached for the glove box and found some tissues, which she used to wipe tears from her face and clean the running mascara.

"Look at you. When did you grow up on me? Boys your age don't speak like that."

Jonas shrugged. "Let's go, Mama. I want to get home. And please drive carefully. No more red lights, right?"

Mary Jo got back on the road and proceeded to drive the six miles which separated Alvin's town centre from their farm. She turned on the radio and the soothing voice of Hank Williams came up. Jonas started singing. They had left town, and ahead of them were only fields of green and blue skies.

Since Harry had left them, two years earlier, managing the farm and taking care of Jonas had been hard. The kid loved his Dad and had struggled to understand why he'd left him. The boys in school, especially Billy Masterson, kept picking on him, and Jonas used his strong fists to argue with them.

But the farm was operating, barely producing enough to pay the mortgage though, and Jonas had been forced to somehow mature a lot faster than expected, being the man of the house and all. Today had been just another incident.

She only hoped these would stop one day.

"Life is good again," thought Mary Jo. *"But for how much longer"?*

June 1964 – Brooklyn, New York

"Come on buddy, give me fifty more. Those abs must be like rock for the fight. This kid will keep hitting your mid-section all night long."

Ace O'Brien was sitting on an upside-down bucket, sucking smoke from his pipe and yelling instructions at Jonas, laying on the mat next to him. He was on the wrong side of forty, meaning he looked no younger than sixty. Boxing since he was thirteen years old, Jonas' trainer had taken quite a few beatings in his professional career, and he had the face and body to prove it.

"Fifty! I'm done, Ace."

Jonas stood up and took his drenched shirt off. He felt his abs burning and he could sense his temples pumping as his heart tried to return back to a normal beat. A woman stared at the young man's half naked body from the other side of the gym and quickly approached him. Jonas was about to put on a fresh shirt but chose not to.

"Jonas Buck, is it?"

"Yes, ma'am. What can I do for you?" Jonas ran his hand over his long blond hair and put on his innocent boy face. He couldn't avoid flirting, and this woman deserved every bit of his big boy charm.

"I'm Caroline Spiegel, from *The Brooklyn Examiner,* and I'll be covering the event tonight. How are you preparing for the fight? I promise I won't tell Manny." Now she was the one flirting, throwing her long black hair from side to side and slightly biting her lower lip.

"My strategy, as recommended by Ace here, is to let him hit me on my mid-section for as long as I can take it. Playing a defensive role and throwing the occasional jabs. This will have him tired by the fifth round or so. Then I'll surprise him with a full-frontal attack. I'll be relentless and he won't have the strength to defend himself. I'll knock him out in the sixth round. Hey, this is confidential information. No telling Manny, right?"

As much as Jonas was being cocky and sounded like he was in total control, he was scared. He was always scared before a fight, but tonight he was facing Manny Suarez, a kid from Venezuela who was unbeaten in twenty fights, all of them by knockout. Jonas' record was seventeen and two, and both losses came against Latin boxers. He would never say this out loud, but he was shit scared of them. Those guys fought like they needed to prove something.

"If you buy me a drink, I promise to keep my mouth shut," she said.

"Well, since you're blackmailing me, I have no options but to comply with your request," replied Jonas.

Ace interrupted the conversation.

"Hang on a second, there will be no blackmailing and no drinks today. You may bang the lady tomorrow, but no alcohol or sex today, Jonas. Is that clear?"

"Well, seems like your daddy got upset. I'll leave you then to continue training. See ya tonight champ!" Caroline left the gym making a gesture like a zipper closing across her lips.

"You can't help yourself kid, can you? C'mon let's do a bit of sparring."

Jonas finally put a new shirt on and obeyed his coach.

January 1960 – Brooklyn, New York

A SAVIOUR WILL ARRIVE TO YOUR LIFE SOON. FOLLOW HIM, LISTEN TO HIM.

Jonas stared at the graffiti, written on a wall inside the station, next to the ticket booth. It looked like it was meant for him. And maybe it was.

He curled onto himself in a section of Greenery Park Station no one ever visited. It was an old tunnel which had been closed off for some reason or other. Not that it was particularly warm, but he could sleep in it without being bothered by the police. He was hungry. The last meal he had was a stolen apple from the grocery store above the station earlier that day.

He woke up at six thirty in the morning, with the rumbling of trains and the sound of commuters walking up and down the corridors.

He sat against a wall in the main station's thoroughfare and placed a hat in front of him, waiting for coins, or even a bill or two. People sped past him, not noticing him or each other.

An hour passed before someone dropped a few pennies. He didn't have to see them to know what type of coins they were. He had learned the noise pennies made when banging against each other. It was a dull sound. Quarters clinked. Quarters were a luxury.

It was late morning when a dollar bill floated down

into his hat. He looked up and saw an old man. He was tall and strong and had a menacing face full of scars.

"Thanks, sir. God bless you."

The man nodded and left.

At the end of the day, Jonas had collected five dollars in his hat. Just enough to buy himself a hot dog and a soda at the street vendor. Maybe an apple.

Jonas thought about how warm it would be at home in Texas. And how his mother would cook his favourite meal of steak and fries, accompanied by a thick chocolate milkshake.

He walked around the subway station and stared at the Brooklyn Bridge towering over the Hudson. Thousands of people walked past Jonas and each other in the busy Brooklyn streets. People talking without speaking. People hearing without listening. People writing songs that no one ever shared. He was lonely alright, but no more than all those citizens aimlessly roaming the streets around them.

He thought about his mother. Good old Mary Josephine Buck. A devout Catholic; a convinced creationist; a woman who couldn't cope with her husband abandoning her. Another solitary soul who preferred to swallow a bullet than to face a lifetime of loneliness.

When Jonas returned to the station, preparing for a cold night, he saw another graffiti on the same wall, near the ticket booth.

YOUR LIFE IS ABOUT TO CHANGE.
EMBRACE THE CHANGE,
DON'T LET YOUR PAST KEEP YOU AWAY FROM SUCCESS.

Another message from the subway prophet.

"Hello darkness, my only friend, I've come to talk with you again. I will be sharing another night with you."

Jonas said these words every night in the blackness of his refuge at the station. A prayer of sorts. In Texas, he used to recite the Lord's prayer before sleeping. In New York, he only spoke to the subway tunnels, and his Bible was graffiti from a faceless prophet.

That night, he dreamed of his mother back in Texas, driving over footpaths and narrowly escaping being crushed while going through a red light. He dreamed about the pot roast she prepared on Sundays after they returned from mass. He dreamed about his dad, who went from cheering him throughout all his baseball games during weekends, to doing his best impersonation of Harry Houdini.

Then he dreamed of the subway prophet. In Jonas' dream, he was a distinguished old man in a robe and grey beard who spoke with a British accent. For some reason, his mind transformed the prophet into Laurence Olivier.

"Your life is about to change … follow him … forget about your past."

He woke up the next morning, hungry and cold as usual.

The same routine as every other day. People passing by in a hurry, ignoring him, the others, and the world surrounding them. The clink of quarters and the dull thud of pennies against each other. Then, a dollar bill, butterflying down to the bottom of the hat.

The man with the scarred face was staring at him. He reminded Jonas of the old man from the TV show *Bonanza*, Ben Cartwright.

"Thanks, sir. Much appreciated."

"What's your name, son?"

"Jonas. Jonas Buck, sir, from Alvin, Texas."

"What the hell are you doing here in the middle of winter freezing your ass off?"

"Had to leave Texas when my mom died last year. We lost our house to the bank. I thought I'd find a good job here in New York but have found nothing yet."

"Tell you what. Come with me and I may find you something to do. You're young and look strong and I could use you in my gym."

Jonas hesitated, but just for a second. He had nowhere to go, no job in sight, and knew no one in this city. If the Bonanza man turned out to be a pervert, Jonas would give him a good ass kicking. The man's face sure showed he had taken a beating or two in his life.

The old man with the marked face and the young man with the ragged clothes left the train station and headed for the 94th Avenue gym.

"… follow him, listen to him."

Jonas could hear the words of the prophet, Laurence Olivier in a robe, loud and clear. Maybe his future rested on the shoulders of the Bonanza man.

JULY 1962 – Brooklyn, New York

Jonas was sparring with Nuke Newton, the best boxer in *Iron Fists,* which was Ace's gym.

Ace, previously nicknamed "Bonanza" by Jonas, was a retired boxer who now trained kids from the five boroughs and made professional fighters out of them. Not many ended up having long careers in boxing. This was a tough sport, and making a living with the fists wasn't easy. Most of them had day jobs.

"Come on kid. Gloves up. Let's see if you are fit enough to spar with me." Nuke was a cocky bastard and knew he was the alpha boy in the place.

"Sure, Nuke, give it to me," replied Jonas.

Jab, jab, left hook, right uppercut. Nuke was fast but Jonas was able to block everything.

"What do you think, kid? Are you prepared for a battery of punches? Let me know if it hurts."

"Bring it on, Nuke."

Jab, hook, uppercut. None of these made Jonas flinch. He saw all of the punches coming and when they landed on his body not much damage was done.

"How 'bout it, Jonas? You want me to stop, or can you take a bit more?"

"What's this guy on about? Boy, I'd like to hit him back," thought Jonas, but continued to do his job and only receive punches and throw occasional jabs to Nuke's face.

"Come on, Nuke, show the kid how it's done!" another boxer yelled from the small crowd gathered around the ring. A bunch of the other boxers followed with similar requests. "Kill him, Nuke," or "Finish him off, buddy," could be heard, pumping up the golden boy.

"Okay, boy, I'm sorry but I think this will hurt."

Nuke started a barrage of punches to Jonas' torso and face. Jab, hook, cross and uppercuts. Jonas was surprised at all the followers cheering Nuke, thinking this was great boxing and making this clown think he was fast and powerful.

Until he had enough.

Jonas easily avoided a wide hook to his face with a quick movement of his head and in a decision made in milliseconds, he landed a strong cross on Nuke's unprotected jaw, stopping him cold. Jonas saw his opponent's body freeze, his eyes rolled inside the skull and his legs collapse. Nuke's body slammed onto the tarp face first. Classic one punch knockout.

The cheering crowd went mute and for the first time since he arrived at the gym, they saw him as a boxer, not as the water boy with a good body who served as a sparring partner to others.

Ace jumped in to the ring and quickly removed Nuke's mouthpiece. Water was poured on his face, and Nuke's eyes rolled back into a normal position. The guy was still unconscious and couldn't stand up. It took four men to drag him out of the ring and into a stretcher.

"Meet me in my office. Now," said Ace to Jonas after leaving Nuke in the hands of the nurse.

Ace closed the door behind him, and the rest of the people in the gym stayed behind the door, eager to know what was up next.

"Listen, Ace, I'm sorry, I know I'm just there to spar, but…"

"You did good, kid. I know you were there only as a sparring partner, but I've never seen Nuke hit the ground before. He's supposed to be a tough fighter and can take a punch, but what I saw there was raw power. I've been watching you for the past few months, and I think you're ready to fight."

"Gee, thanks. I also think I am. Just say when and where."

"There's a bit of work to do before your first fight. You have just landed one punch in your boxing life. It's not like you are the new Cassius Clay."

For the next six months, Ace concentrated on teaching Jonas how to box. He was a natural and had the gift of brutal power, but he needed to learn a lot more and be exposed to professional boxers.

Ace paid a hundred dollars to a man from New Jersey named Vito. He was a bouncer at a night club and worked for the D'Amore family, who controlled the construction unions in New York.

"Hey, Ace. This is a mountain of a man. What's his

weight?" asked a nervous Jonas when he stepped into the ring and had a look at his opponent.

"I believe he stopped the scales at two hundred and forty pounds."

"Are you fucking kidding me? That's more than sixty pounds above my weight! Why couldn't you get me someone my own size?"

"Do you want to fight or prefer to go back to cleaning toilets and be Nuke's sparring bitch? Be a man and take this bastard down. I only paid for three rounds, so better make the best of it."

The bell sounded and both men got into it. Vito's long arms kept Jonas from getting too close to him. The first blow was landed by the Italian to Jonas' right ear, making him stumble and retreat onto a corner. Then Vito came to Jonas like a beast, preparing his right hand for a massive blow. When the Italian's right arm was extended to the fullest, trying to gain as much thrust as possible, he left his face unprotected. Jonas then landed a battery of six jabs, which made Vito fall on his ass, not knowing what had hit him.

The big guy stood up, and Jonas saw anger on the man's face. The anger of a Mafia henchman whose pride was hurt. But Jonas was now sure he could beat this guy, no matter his weight.

Vito lunged at Jonas, with all of his two hundred and forty pounds wanting to crush this insolent pretty boy. But Jonas was too fast. He avoided the several punches thrown at him, as he saw them coming in slow motion.

Had Vito landed just one of these hooks, Jonas would have surely gone flying over the ropes.

But Vito barely touched Jonas' body.

During the third round, Vito got tired. He couldn't move, and his arms grew heavy. Midway into the round, Jonas attacked his opponent mercilessly with hooks to his abdomen. Vito curled and tried to protect his body with his arms, and when Jonas saw the opportunity, he landed an uppercut right to the man's jaw, turning his switch off. Game over.

"Good job tonight, boy. To be honest, I never thought you would beat Vito. I've seen this man fight before and let me tell you, I never saw him on the ground. In fact, I had twenty bucks on him beating you," said Ace while he removed the gloves from Jonas' hand in the locker room.

"Thanks for your vote of confidence. It's very reassuring."

That night Jonas left the gym with a sense of accomplishment. For two years he had worked at the gym for Ace and had developed a strong body by lifting weights and training with the boxers, but he was still the new boy from Texas who cleaned the toilets. Now he had one fight under his belt. Not official of course but beating a man so much heavier than him had to account for something.

He walked into the alleyway which led to his apartment building and saw a message written on the wall.

THIS MAY BE THE FIRST STEP IN YOUR NEW LIFE.
DON'T LET THIS GO TO WASTE.

Jonas smiled. These words were repeated by the prophet who lived in his head morphed into Laurence Olivier.

He had no plans on wasting anything.

June 1964 – Manhattan, New York

"Hello darkness my old friend."

Jonas was sitting on a bench in Central Park, praying to the night. The fight was in an hour, and he needed his time alone, away from the noise of the arena. He didn't like the crowds, so he preferred to stay away from the sights and sounds of the boxing scene for as long as he could before a fight.

He stared into the blackness of the night, reflecting on his life.

When he had arrived in New York from Texas, he had quickly realised that the big city was not what he expected. While he was growing up, he thought New York was this dreamland of opportunities where he would easily find a good paying job and women would jump at him just by wearing his cowboy hat. What he found was a cold place, packed with heartless humans who tried to live ignoring everyone around them, people who bowed and prayed to a neon God who lived in Times Square.

When Ace took him under his arm, he spent a year or so with him before he could afford his own matchbox rental apartment. He loved Ace, but he preferred to be alone. And even though he had many romantic adventures, his relationships ended at the crack of dawn after he had sex. One of his colleagues at the gym asked him once: "Hey Jonas, what is the definition of a great relationship for you?" to which he replied: "Two nights."

Jonas walked back to the Jefferson Heights Arena, the gym which hosted tonight's event. As he approached the place, the roar of the crowd grew. The third fight of the program was on, and two Puerto Rican kids were belting each other to the amusement of a packed house.

"The Prodigal Son has returned, Hallelujah." Ace was pissed, as usual, by Jonas's pre-fight disappearance.

"Come on, old boy. Just strap me up. Let's do this," Jonas was now talking himself up. There was a lot on the line for him that night.

Ace and Shorty strapped Jonas's arm and rubbed his biceps, warming his muscles.

"Remember this, son, you are a much better fighter than Manny. He's loud and flashy, and can run around the ring like a deer, but he gets tired after five. Just protect your face and let him try to hurt your body until he is tired. You can do this, kid."

Ace and his famous short pep-talks. Jonas was used to them. But he was right. That was the way to beat Manny.

Or at least this is what he wanted to believe.

At exactly 10 p.m. both boxers stepped into the ring. Manny Suarez brought with him a large entourage of Latin supporters who danced to a salsa tune while walking towards the ring, all of them wearing colourful shirts and dangling gold chains. To Jonas, they looked and moved like the Sharks, the gang in the hit movie West Side Story. If Jonas had had more followers, they could have been the Jets, but his group only included Ace and the limping stocky man known as Shorty.

Manny was a handsome fellow with long and curly hair and a pencil moustache. The ultimate Latin lover. The press had a feast announcing this as a battle of races and suburbs. Manny from the Bronx against the white hope from Brooklyn. If Jonas had been Irish or Italian, the headlines would have been extraordinary.

"You've got this, big boy."

Jonas looked down from the ring and saw Caroline, the reporter, sitting in one of the ring side seats, notepad in hand. She was indeed a gorgeous woman.

"Come to the change rooms after the fight," mouthed Jonas, hoping she could hear him.

"Will do," was her short reply, which came with a seductive wink.

The fight started and Manny started doing Manny things. He ran around the ring, throwing well timed jabs which frequently landed on Jonas' head. Jonas tried to corner him, but the salsa dancing boxer was too slippery. The crowd was largely in favour of the popular Manny.

Rounds were mounting. Two, three, four and five, and Manny kept doing his dance and scoring points with the judges, while Jonas kept his head down, took punches to the body, and waited for Manny to get tired. But perhaps Manny was better prepared for this fight than Jonas and Ace had expected.

After the sixth round's bell sounded, Jonas was the one who was exhausted.

"Ace, I think Manny didn't read your script man. He's not one bit tired!" said Jonas while gasping for air.

"I know. The fucker must have trained on his endurance. I've never seen him in such good form."

"Man, I'm fucking tired. I don't how much more I have in the tank. What should I do?"

"There's only four rounds to go, but you are so down in points you'll never win that way. You need to go for the knockout. Now."

"Fuck me. This guy is very slippery and I'm tired."

"It's your only chance, boy," Shorty said. "A good uppercut to his chin and he will be dancing salsa in a hospital bed." This was the only time Shorty opened his mouth during the fight.

The bell rang announcing the start of the seventh round.

Jonas stood up slowly, and Manny ran towards him with his fists up and rage in his eyes.

June 1964 – Brooklyn, New York

Jonas woke up still dizzy from the fight. Sure, Manny didn't hit too hard, but Jonas had taken at least two hundred blows to his head and torso, and this morning he felt each one of them.

"Hey champ. Good morning. I tried cooking breakfast without waking you up, but this apartment is so small It's impossible not to. How did you sleep?" said Caroline.

"I blacked out completely. Haven't been that tired in my life."

"Well, that Manny looked like Speedy Gonzalez up there, you could barely catch him."

The couple had breakfast in bed. Scrambled eggs with bacon and toast. Caroline was lucky. This was the only meal she could prepare, and Jonas happened to have the three ingredients in his miniature kitchen. Single twenty-something people wanting to live in New York, trying to climb up the socio-economic ladder, did the best they could to survive every day with as little as they could.

"What are you going to write in your article today? I'm curious," asked Jonas.

"Massive upset at the Heights. Little known Brooklyn boy ends fight with a seventh-round knockout of fan favourite Manny Suarez. What do you think?"

"Don't like the 'little known' part. People do know me. I think."

"Ace, Shorty, and your gym buddies don't count. Sorry, I forgot, you don't have any buddies."

"Very funny. But I don't care. That's who I am. Maybe you can give me a nickname, something that sticks now that I'll be fighting with upper tier guys."

"What about The Texas Bomber?"

"Yeah, I like the sound of that."

"The Texas Bomber it is. And what nickname would you give me?" asked Caroline.

"Three nights," replied Jonas and chuckled.

That evening Jonas went out around Brooklyn, alone as usual, and strolled along the Hudson where many people were walking. Some by themselves, others in couples, a few more in larger groups. For some reason people seemed to be happy and enjoying the warm summer night. They crowded the ice cream and hot dog vendors, and some had brought their kids along. People were talking with each other. He didn't see the rush of other occasions.

Jonas sat in his usual bench, overlooking the bridge, until the rest of the world around him faded away.

"Hello darkness, my old friend. I've come to talk with you again."

"And what would you talk about?"

Caroline's voice startled him. She felt alone in the apartment and knew where to look for him. She hoped she wasn't being too intrusive after only one night together.

"Tonight, I would have talked about my career, about life, and about you."

"Who's stopping you?"

He looked at her. There was something special about this woman. Something which he was willing to discover.

"No one. I've just realised I don't need to do this anymore."

STARRY NIGHT

After Don McLean

February 1891, Paris

"Theo, what should I do?"

The young woman stared at the crates. There were several of them occupying most of the once spacious living room.

A cruel reminder of what had caused her husband's death at thirty-three years of age, Johanna's instinct was to get rid of them.

Johanna lifted the lid from one of the crates and pulled out a painting. There must have been at least a hundred of them in the wooden box. Her brother-in-law had been a prolific painter, but he was also a troubled soul. His work had never been taken seriously. Theo was the only one who believed in his talent, but his judgment was clouded by the love he felt for his older brother.

She heard her baby boy crying in his bedroom and quickly attended to him, taking the painting with her.

"Hush, hush, Vinnie. Mum is here."

The infant's face brightened when he saw his mother and felt the familiar warmth of her chest while she prepared to feed him.

She looked out the window while the baby sucked and saw families having picnics by the Seine on a sunny Sunday. A man with a straw hat and twisting moustache was flying a multicolour kite while twin girls in matching blue dresses danced around him. The mother was sitting on the grass, and, in the centre of a red and white checked blanket, a wicker basket was open. Johanna imagined cheese, jam, biscuits, and bread plus a bottle or two of wine were packed inside.

When finished, Johanna burped Vincent and sat him on her lap, resting against her chest.

Johanna looked at the painting, which she had placed on the sofa. The baby stared at it, as if he understood what was painted. Or maybe it was the intensity of the yellow sunflowers that caught his attention. Perhaps these paintings could be sold to schools, she thought, trying to find an excuse not to throw them away.

"Theo, what should I do?"

December 1888, Arles

"Dear Theo,

Everything is in shambles. My plans of starting an artist's commune with Paul are a total failure. Paul is too arrogant and doesn't respect my art. He also accused me, and for that matter yourself, of taking financial advantage of him. Last night we yelled at each other, and he left the house. I tried to convince him to return, but to no avail. I was told this morning that he accused me of chasing him down the street with a razor. I have no recollection of such actions. But you know me, sometimes I have these blackouts and can't remember a thing. I'm going to need your support, my beloved brother.

Vincent"

"My dearest Vincent,

I have been told by Doctor Rey that the infection to your wound has been controlled and that you don't feel pain anymore. He asked me to insist that you let them clean it and change the bandage every few days. I loved the portrait of the Doctor that you painted in your last letter. He is a kind man who looks after you, my dear brother, so I beg you to listen to him. I will be visiting you on Christmas Day, as I have not seen you in ages.

Yours always… Theo."

When the 9 am train from Paris arrived, Vincent was at the platform, anxious to see his brother for the first time since he had moved to Arles. Even though they wrote to each other frequently, daily at times, they had not met in person in several months.

"Here he is. So great to see you, little brother. I have missed you so much."

Theo hugged Vincent and could not speak, overwhelmed with the sadness of seeing a loved one in such a poor condition. The bandage covering Vincent's ear was bloody and filthy. He was extremely thin, and his pale blue eyes seemed dark and had sunken into his skull.

"I love you, Vincent. You need to remember that always. I'm only a train ride away, and if you feel lonely you can come to Paris and stay with me."

"How can I not remember when you keep telling me this in your letters? Come on, I need to show you what I've been up to."

During the walk to the Yellow House, where Vincent lived, they saw peasants working the fields, endless expanses of yellow and green with irises in bloom, and white houses with orchards. In the township of Arles, they walked along the main street.

"This is the Café Terrace. I come here frequently, and every other day they throw me out. I seem to upset the patrons. Gerard, the owner, keeps saying he will ban me from ever coming again, but never does. People enjoy watching the crazy painter quarrel with everyone. I give this bloody sleepy village something to see." Vincent laughed, but Theo only saw emptiness behind his brother's laughter.

They arrived at the Yellow House.

Theo saw portraits hung in empty halls and frameless heads on empty walls, with eyes that watch this world from Vincent's own universe.

In his bedroom there were dozens, maybe hundreds, of paintings and drawings. Theo recognized the peasants harvesting, the orchards they had just walked past, and the Café Terrace. The fields, buildings and streets of Arles were all documented in canvases with Vincent's peculiar thick lines and bright colours. The same style that Theo tried to sell in Paris but was frowned upon by the critics and art experts.

"And this is for you, my dear brother. Merry Christmas."

On an easel, the paint still fresh, there was a blue and grey painting of a night in Arles, with the silhouette of the houses and the church in the night. Stars and planets were lighting up the sky as beautiful clouds swirled about. The beauty of the painting overwhelmed Theo, who couldn't hold back tears.

"I know you'll probably think this painting doesn't have market value, but you need to know I had you in my thoughts when I painted it. There is a part of me in this one Theo. Every time you look at it, think that I am in one of these houses."

"I'm lost for words, Vincent. This is the most beautiful of all your paintings. I will keep it with me until my death."

That night, the brothers went to the Café Terrace for dinner and drinks. Gerard, the owner, was polite with them.

"Gerard, this is my brother, Theo. He came to visit from Paris."

"Pleased to meet you, Theo. Vincent talks about you all the time. That is, when he's not harassing other clients here." Gerard chuckled. Theo couldn't see the angry man his brother told him about.

"Nice meeting you, Gerard. You have a fine place here, so fine that Vincent keeps painting it from all angles."

A shot was heard in the distance.

"Bloody hunters. They keep shooting deer even when the hunting season is over," said Gerard, changing into the cranky man Vincent was used to.

They had a quiet dinner, although Gerard kept an eye on Vincent whenever other people sat at a nearby table.

After eating Vincent walked Theo to the train station, along the same fields outside Arles they had walked past earlier in the day.

"You know something, Theo? I met a stranger in these fields once. A magic day he passed my way, and though we talked of many things, fools and kings, this he said to me: The greatest thing you'll ever learn is just to love and be loved in return. Isn't that brilliant?"

That Christmas night Theo returned to Paris with the painting under his arm, an emptiness in his heart, and not knowing if he would ever see his brother alive again.

July 1890, St. Remy

Vincent scanned the landscape ahead of him. The sun had just set but the horizon still flashed orange and yellow beams into the sky, remnants of sunlight slowly but aggressively being swallowed by the darkness of the night.

It was that precise moment when the day lost its identity, not knowing whether it was day or night. The time when Vincent's sinister thoughts flourished. The time when episodes of loss accosted him.

He remembered beautiful Kee, his cousin in Etten, seven years his senior, with whom a younger Vincent was obsessed. Her words in reply to his marriage proposal—*"No, nay, never"*—still hurt nine years later.

Sien, his lover while in The Hague. The woman who left prostitution for him, and whose daughter Vincent treated like his own. Sien modelled and gave his life a sense of stability. He cursed the day he abandoned her, pressured by his family due to her reputation. Sien returned to prostitution, gave away her children, and killed herself.

Vincent thought of Rachel, whom he had met at the brothel in Arles, and who patiently listened to his stories of despair. Vincent thought she deserved to have a piece of himself, so he gave her his ear believing she would cherish this precious gift.

He also remembered Gaugin, with whom Vincent thought of creating a painters' commune in Arles. Paul Gaugin, his best friend, his creative soulmate, a genius with unlimited talent who understood and appreciated his art. Both men shared a house for a few months and created masterpieces together, until Vincent tried to hurt him with a razor, forcing Gaugin to leave.

"Why did you even think of marrying me, Vincent? We were cousins, and I was grieving for my husband."

"Why did you leave me, alone with my daughter and son, so I had to become a prostitute again? You made me kill myself, Vincent."

"Why did you think giving me a bloody chopped ear would make me happy, Vincent?"

"Why did you chase me down the road with a razor, Vincent? I thought we were friends and had an artistic bond."

Angry faces and recriminating voices waiting for that time of the day when Vincent was at his most vulnerable.

It was finally night-time, and with the darkness came the beautiful views of Arles under a clear sky and a full moon. Planets and stars above illuminated the silhouette of the church and buildings in town.

It was the time when he thought about Theo, the only person who loved him for what he was. The one who was always there, offering him support, admiring his art and understanding his loneliness.

Vincent wept. He realised how much his brother meant to him, and felt ungrateful for not being a better brother, a better friend.

He looked at the sky and mumbled. *"Starry, starry night, fill my pallet with blue and grey. Let's pray for a bright summer's day, with eyes that know the sadness in my soul."*

It was a still night at the Café Terrace.

With the warm weather and clear skies, the chairs outside the café were filled with patrons eating and drinking.

That was when the shot was heard.

"Bloody hunters. There won't be a deer alive in the whole province soon," said Gerard from his place behind the bar.

July 1890, St. Remy

"Vincent, it's me, Theo. Can you hear me?"

A pair of blue eyes opened to the world and the first thing they saw was the familiar face of his younger brother. Vincent smiled, but to the eyes of those around him his face remained still.

"I'm not sure he can hear you," said doctor Gachet, while a nurse in an impossibly white uniform removed the dressings on his chest, exposing a terrible wound. Charred skin surrounded a black bullet hole, which seemed to lead to an empty void inside Vincent's body.

"Is he going to live, doctor?" asked an anxious Theo.

"The bullet went through his chest without causing major damage to any organs other than the lung, but he has lost too much blood. He arrived on foot at the hospital yesterday and since then he has been in and out of consciousness. This is the first time he has opened his eyes since last night. I'm afraid he doesn't have much time left."

"Hey, big brother. Why did you do this? You could have come to Paris and stayed with me and Johanna. I have a good feeling about your paintings. People are starting to warm up to your style."

Vincent could see his brother and listen to him, but he had no strength to talk or move any part of his dying body. Theo's words were meant to make him feel good.

His brother, his beautiful brother, always trying to cheer him up. But no one understood him, not even Theo. No one knew the pain he felt. The pain of loving too much but not being loved back. The pain of people not understanding what he was trying to say to the world through his paintings.

In the middle of his comatose state, the physical pain disappeared, and everything became calm. He could not hear Theo anymore. He saw blurry figures hovering over him, doing something to his body, and the image of the stranger he met at the fields of Arles appeared, taking everything else out of Vincent's view.

The stranger with whom he talked of many things, of fools and kings.

The stranger who said, "The greatest thing you'll ever learn is just to love and to be loved in return."

Vincent then began to move his right hand, grabbed Theo by the arm, and, with a force which was unexpected from a man in his condition, he pulled his brother close to him.

"The sadness will last forever," were the last words he muttered before leaving this world.

July 1890, Auvers

"We are gathered here to say farewell to Vincent van Gogh," Father Rochard said. "Although a troubled soul, he had a big heart and was in an eternal quest for love. Love from his family, friends and his fellow artists. He was also looking for perfection in his art. Vincent refused to paint following the rules and standards expected by the critics. He had his own and unique style and wanted everyone to understand his world through his paintings. I have been blessed to be in his company and to witness his creative process. Everyone in Arles and St. Remy became accustomed to seeing Vincent with his easel, painting in the middle of the wheat fields, or just passing by, absorbing the views of these places to create his paintings. Let us pray for the eternal rest of Vincent van Gogh's soul."

Father Rochard said a prayer, and the people gathered around the coffin repeated his words.

Theo was surprised at the number of attendants, which included artists like Pissarro and Laval, Doctor Gachet, some twenty family members and dozens of locals.

Gerard approached Theo and gave him a hug and his condolences.

"I know he told you I kept booting him out of the restaurant. I had to. Sometimes he went on a rage and scared people. But I knew he had goodness in his heart.

I'm no doctor but I'm sure some demons in his head awakened from time to time and he couldn't tame them. I'm sorry for your loss." The hardened man was weeping.

Maybe Vincent had, unknowingly, reached the hearts of many people in his own weird way. Maybe not. It was also possible that locals were just curious about the funeral of the crazy Dutch painter.

When the crowd dispersed, Theo stayed alone, looking down at the coffin which was already lowered into the hole and partially covered with dirt. He pulled a folded piece of paper from his breast pocket and read aloud, to no one but himself.

"I think I understand what you tried to say to me. How you struggled with your sanity, trying to set your feelings free. No one listened, maybe they didn't know how. Hopefully, they'll listen now."

February 1891, Paris

Johanna put Vinnie back in his cot. He was asleep again.

The afternoon grew colder, and families left their picnic spots for the warmth of their homes. From the window, Johanna could see the street vendors closing shop for the day. Some of these were artists who painted replicas of Monet's lilies or Degas' ballet dancers. She imagined one of these street painters copying Vincent's paintings. Maybe the Sunflowers or the Starry Night. One of his many self-portraits even. But that was pure fantasy. Theo had no luck in promoting Vincent in Paris.

Johanna started the fireplace as the house was getting colder by the minute. She poured herself a glass of brandy and started pulling out paintings from the crates, placing them side by side. There were so many, and from the very different styles Vincent tried in his life.

Her gaze moved from a self-portrait of Vincent with a bandaged ear to the church in Auvers; from a Japanese style painting to a portrait of Doctor Gachet; from a prisoner's round in jail to the old man weeping in his chair.

Johanna realised she had absorbed Vincent's life through his art, as explained by Theo.

But in the words of the critics, Vincent's paintings were not worth more than the replicas of Monet which were sold in the streets of Paris.

After Vincent's death, Theo's sorrow turned him into a

sad and hollow man. He used to enjoy taking Vinnie and Johanna for walks along the river and was passionate about his job as an arts dealer. He always saw the bright side of life. But he suffered in silence for his brother, desperate to find a way to keep his spirits high and frustrated for not finding a way to do so. Theo was constantly worried about Vincent taking his own life.

Six months after Vincent's death, weak and unable to cope with his brother's passing, Theo died.

"I cannot force you to keep the paintings, Jo. Do whatever you want with them. Hopefully you will find someone who appreciates them and makes Vincent famous. It's up to you, but please give my brother at least a chance."

Johanna always thought of getting rid of the paintings in one way or another. Giving them away would have been easy. But she blamed Theo's death on Vincent and his art, so another part of her wanted to burn them.

"Theo, Theo, what should I do?"

When Johanna started picking up the paintings and putting them back in the crates, she realised the only one that was hung on a wall in their house was the Starry Night, Theo's favourite. She took the painting down from its place above the fireplace. Before putting it into one of the crates, she noticed there was a paper stuck to the back of the painting. It had Theo's handwriting.

"Those you loved wouldn't love you,
Even though your love was true,

And when no hope was left in sight,
On that bright and starry night
You took your life, as I feared you would do,
As I always told you, Vincent,
This world was never meant for
Someone as wonderful as you."

Johanna cried in silence when she read these words, which Theo had never shared with her.

At that moment she decided she would do whatever she could to tell the world the story of Vincent van Gogh through his paintings.

God, would someone ever be interested in his art?

It's Gonna Be a Long, Long Time

After Elton John

July 1975

Dust. Red dust.

All Tom could see from the control room windows was red dust.

This particular storm was now entering its first month, and it had been weeks since the last time he had taken the rover out.

Tom did, however, like the sound of the storm hitting the surface of the pods. It was irregular, not following any kind of pattern, and broke the monotony of his life on the planet.

When the storm went into one of its quiet lapses, he caught a glimpse of Pod No.2, its silver coned top showing hints of damage. A few panels would need replacing soon. He could not determine how the top of Pod No.1 looked like as the cameras above were covered with dust.

"Morning, AIMS. Please give me a status on Pod No.2," he said.

"Morning, Thomas. All systems in Pod No.2 remain operational. The damage to Linkway No.1 has not affected either end," replied the Artificial Intelligence Management System in a woman's voice from overhead.

"HOLO?"

"The HOLO system is in perfect condition, Thomas."

"How much longer before I need to repair the crack to the linkway?"

"Pod No.2 can continue unattended for twelve more weeks, so I suggest you do not risk going out there to do any repairs until then. Chances of survival outside in these conditions are 9%"

"Thanks, AIMS."

"Do you want the results of Major League Baseball? The Orioles have won again against the Yankees. Brilliant performance by Jim Palmer."

"Just print the results. I'll check them out later."

Tom went back to his room and laid down on the bed. He missed his family, and could not use HOLO. Outside, the storm had regained force and the battering sound made him doze off into a non-existent Mars night.

July 1972

"We are go for flight, gents. Godspeed."

Tom looked to his right and saw Les, who only had eyes for the monitors above them, completely frozen, almost catatonic, not even blinking. To his left, Chris was checking the readings for the tenth time, repeating figures out loud. Each was managing stress in a different way. This is the part where Tom felt left out, like the unwanted third wheel in a weird three-way relationship. Chris was the experienced astronaut, with three missions on his resume. Les was the Captain, and had only been in one mission before, but it was the one that left the Mothership orbiting the Earth. Between both, they had accumulated over sixty hours of EVA. Tom was just the scientist, the geek who knew how to grow vegetables. Whoohoo.

The crackling voice from Houston started the countdown.

10 … 9 … 8 … 7… 6 … 5 … 4 … 3… 2… 1 … 0.

Tom was deafened by the roar of a hundred thousand gallons of fuel exploding under him, and the fifteen-stories-high spacecraft shook violently while taking off. The G force generated by the Saturn VI rocket sledgehammered him to his seat. He prayed, the same way he did every time he was on a plane during take-off, asking God to give his wife Pam and daughter Joy strength in case something went wrong. Now that the candle was lit, his life was not in his hands anymore.

Once they left the atmosphere, everything went quiet. No roar, no shaking, no sledgehammer.

"That was some launch. Hey, Les. What do you think?" asked Chris.

"Much stronger than last time. And shakier," replied Les. Tom looked at her. She even blinked.

"Agree. This Saturn VI rocket is a beast," said Chris.

Tom had nothing to say. No prior experience, no technical knowledge. He didn't think a comment about the organic tomatoes he was planning to grow would be appropriate at that point.

"How is the view from up there, Captain?" asked the Flight Director from Houston with his deep DJ voice.

"Could not be better, Houston. We can see the earth getting smaller by the minute."

"All readings look good from here. What are you getting over there, Chris?"

"Everything is A-OK Houston. All figures are where they should be."

"Hey, Doctor Bradford, congratulations, you have just lost your launch virginity. You sure you don't need a diaper change?" The voice from Houston was loud and clear, and Tom imagined millions of people around the world laughed. Tom had a regression to the eighth grade, when he was bullied by a large kid with freckles called Ron who used to take his lunch money.

"No, I think I'm good and dry in that department, but thanks for asking, Houston."

July 1975

Tom kept checking the status of the systems in the Control Room. The levels of oxygen, temperature and internal pressure were stable. According to AIMS, all systems and essential readings in Pod No.2 were also stable. These structures had been built to withstand the harsh conditions of the red planet.

"You guys have been behaving well. Look at how much you have grown already," said Tom to the tomatoes, which stared back at him with indifference, not too dissimilar to the looks he used to receive from Les and Chris.

The rate of growth, the weight, and the moisture contents exceeded the numbers in the Green Report, the 600 page document that impressed the President and landed him this gig. He complimented himself, but sadly there was no one to celebrate with. What was the line—"It's lonely out in space."

When he reported back to Houston all he got was a less than enthusiastic "well done." It appeared that after the compound was established and everyone else returned to Earth the mission was finished. No one really gave a damn about a glorified veggie patch.

In fact, back on Earth people were disappointed. The goals of the mission were broadly documented and involved the establishment of a scientific camp. This would be expanded during a 30-year span and aimed to explore the red planet and the possibility of colonization. But common people did not care about such long winded plans. It was like telling a kid who received a toy race car for Christmas that he would have to wait another day so that they could buy batteries for it.

What everyone on Earth really wanted to know was what the Martians really looked like. When it became evident that Mars was an isolated place with a most boring landscape, the media coverage of the mission dwindled to almost zero.

"The vegetables are in perfect condition, Tom. You should be satisfied with this result," the melodious voice of AIMS said from the concealed speakers. Tom was sure that NASA used the voice of a Bond girl for this computer.

"Thanks, AIMS. That was the goal. I wish others were as enthusiastic about this as you are. I'm starting to think you have a crush on me."

"You know I'm here for you, Tom, whenever you need me."

"I know, and thank you for that. These tomatoes are gorgeous, but I don't think they like me very much. They never talk back to me."

"Hahaha, that is funny, Tom. I like your sense of humour."

Tom thought of replying, but having a computer laugh at your joke, even though he thought it was a good one, left him speechless.

October 1972

"Wake up Dr. Bradford. Your hibernation period has ended," said the sexy voice of AIMS.

Tom had been wakening since the system pumped the fluid into his veins a good ten minutes back, but it took him some time to completely regain consciousness. If waking up from an afternoon nap made you feel dazed, imagine coming back from a ninety-day slumber.

"Good morning, I guess. How do you feel?" The beautiful face of Captain Leslie McKay greeted him from her seat in the lounge.

"I've felt better, but to be honest I thought my joints were going to hurt from being stiff for that long."

"Nah, our NASA doctors have thought of everything. Your body was pumped with all sorts of fluids during your sleep, including a bit of oil for the creaky hinges."

"I'm starving. What is there for breakfast, or should I say dinner?"

"Help yourself, buddy." Les pointed at the clear glazed fridge, which looked like a vending machine on steroids. Several dozen tubes, similar to toothpaste containers, were on display offering anything from pizza to a pork roast. Tom grabbed one which promised him a cheeseburger and even had the McDonalds logo on it. He took the cap off, squeezed the tube, and a brown paste slid onto his melamine plate. He inserted it into the instant oven and in one minute the cold ugly brown paste had evolved into a warm ugly brown paste.

Even though the food resembled his own turd, the flavour was not bad at all. He could taste the meat, the bun, the sauce and even the pickles. In a smaller separate tube, he found the fries. Who knew his first meal after a three-month sleep would be a McDonalds combo.

After getting a bath and changing into the official NASA uniform, Tom went straight to the HOLO chamber. His time slot was in a few minutes.

"Okay, AIMS, I'm ready for my session. Fire away," said Tom after taking a seat inside the glass capsule.

"Please relax, Doctor Bradford. You will see a greenish fog filling up the capsule, but it will dissipate rather quickly. Do not try to stand up until I tell you to do so. Here we go."

A soft hiss came from a series of pipes above, and a cold green fog engulfed him. He felt peace.

As the fog cleared he saw Pat and Joy, sitting on the couch in their living room. They were so close he felt tempted to reach out and touch them.

"Here's Daddy! Hi Daddy, can you see me?"

"Yes, I can see you, Joy. Wow, it feels like I'm home next to you!"

"Hi Tommy, we've missed you so much. How was your hibernation?" The voices were loud and clear, and the images perfect. It was hard to believe he was really a million miles away.

"I don't remember much of it. One second, I was

awake, then I closed my eyes and when I opened them again, three months had gone by. And now I'm here, or at least a hologram of myself."

"It's amazing to see you this close, yet you are so far away it makes me sad."

The conversation went on for twenty minutes, the time allocated to each astronaut per week. As soon as it was over, the hologram slowly disintegrated from view back in Texas, like a ghost, leaving Pam and Joy disheartened and Tom with a feeling of emptiness.

"How was the interaction with your family, Doctor Bradford?"

"It was perfect, AIMS. Thanks for arranging. I guess I'll have to wait another week for the next encounter."

Before going to bed, Tom decided to write in his journal. NASA had recommended to keep a diary and write their experiences in it. Tom's first entry in the journal was: *"I miss the Earth too much. I miss my wife and kid. It's lonely out in space. This is such an endless flight."*

That night, the first of the remaining six months of travel, Tom went to sleep with a void in his soul he didn't know how to fill.

December 1975

God Only Knows from the Beach Boys was playing through loudspeakers.

"Thanks, AIMS, you know how to make me feel better," said Tom while keeping his eyes on the numbers in front of him. His weekly report back to Houston was due in a few hours.

Of course, AIMS knew how to make him feel better. The computer had been fed data pertaining to each of the astronauts which included their tastes in music, sports and literature. Because Tom was the only one who would remain in the mission for four years, more attention was paid to him than the others.

"I'm here to serve, Tommy. All I want is to make your stay in this resort more enjoyable."

"Tommy?" thought Tom. There was a big leap from "Doctor Bradford" three years ago to the now familiar "Tommy."

"Do you want to play a game of chess, Tommy?"

"Let me finish the report and I'll be all yours."

"Sounds tempting," replied the computer.

Once the report was finished, AIMS saved it and reported back to Earth by EMS, the electronic mail system designed by IBM exclusively for NASA.

"I'm ready for you, Tommy, let's give this game a go. You play white."

Tom drank a cup of fake wine, and they started playing. After each of Tom's moves, AIMS replied by giving verbal instructions to Tom about her next play.

"Checkmate! I can't believe I beat you. First time in three years. How about that!"

"You are getting better at this game, Tommy. You have finally learned how to beat me. How about another drink?"

"You're on. Let me grab another of these fake wine boxes and we can play again."

AIMS changed the music. The melodic voice of Carole King started singing *It's too late.*

Another twenty minutes and Tom had another checkmate.

"Yay Tommy. You are becoming a genius at this game. I hope you don't want to trade me for a younger computer."

"You crack me up, AIMS. I swear to God, you would make a perfect woman."

"Maybe I already am, Tommy. Don't you think?"

December 1972

"Our first Christmas in space, Tom. What do you make of it?"

"Doesn't feel like one. Without a tree, the reindeers, the lights. My daughter was disguised as an elf when we had our HOLO session earlier. God, how I miss her, and how I miss my wife.

Les and Tom had had HOLO sessions with their families, a special Christmas edition, earlier that day.

"Poor Chris. All frozen and alone. He was a pain in the ass to deal with while you were hibernating Tom, but he's going to be all yours in a couple of weeks."

"You're the lucky one, Les. Hibernating last, to be awakened upon arrival."

"If you say so," replied the Captain.

Tom could not read her very well. She was smart but very sarcastic, with a dry sense of humour. He never knew when she was joking or being serious when they discussed matters unrelated to the mission.

"How was the session with your husband, Les?"

"It was like having a regular after dinner conversation about our days at the office. Full of monosyllables and head nods. We never talk about anything substantial, the same we did at home. At least back then we had sex, which helped me get to sleep."

Another of those comments that Tom could not read.

The only difference was this time he detected watery eyes. Les turned around to avoid his gaze.

"Hey, it's Christmas, Les. Houston gave us a bit of free time. Hi AIMS, would you play some music we could dance to?"

"Sure, Doctor Bradford. Here is Johnny Be Good by Chuck Berry," replied AIMS.

When the first chords of the tune started playing, Tom grabbed Les by the hand and they started dancing, her face lighting up from hearing her favourite artist. They took turns at drinking from the box of wine and clumsily performed zero gravity dance moves.

"Thanks, Tom."

"Thanks for what?"

"For not being an asshole. There's a rule in NASA which states that in each spaceflight there can be only one asshole, and that is Chris. The journey would be much worse if sixty six percent of the astronauts were assholes."

"I'll try my best to play the non-asshole role the rest of the trip, just for you."

"I have one thing to ask you. Come here."

"Yes, what is...."

Tom was silenced by the kiss Les planted on his lips. He felt the wine in her breath and responded to the kiss with passion.

December 1975

"AIMS, I'm going to Pod No.2. The storm has almost dissipated completely. What are the chances of survival?"

"I do not recommend such an action. Chances of survival walking through the damaged link are 35%"

"That can't be correct. A week ago, you gave me the same percentage and Pod No.1 was shaking like crazy under the storm."

Tom changed into the spacesuit and walked towards the hatch that led to the linkway.

"Open the hatch, AIMS. If I see anything I don't like I'll return immediately."

"I do not recommend such an action."

Tom thought about it and decided to do something he had never done before. He returned to the Control Room and from his computer terminal punched a few keys. The command *Disable AIMS* flashed ahead of him. He knew Houston would query him about it, but that was problem for another day. Before he hit the button, AIMS tried to speak.

"Please don't do this, Tommy, let me ----"

The voice of Raquel Welch was muted upon the activation of the command.

He stepped into the airlock and opened the hatch to the linkway. The full length of the round corridor was lit up. Once the hatch closed behind him, Tom checked the pressure, temperature, and oxygen levels with a manual device. The figures came back in green, meaning they were within human survival range. He opened the visor of his helmet and breathed nothing but clean air.

"You're a lying bitch, AIMS," he said.

When he reached Pod No.2, he found out all parameters were normal. Lights were on and monitors on the walls were displaying the Control Room and Herbarium in Pod No.1

Tom went straight to the HOLO chamber. It was six PM in Arlington, and usually at this time Pam would be in the kitchen, having dinner with Joy or doing the dishes. Pam would not be expecting him, so the chances of meeting with them were not good.

He settled, punched the commands, jumped into the chamber and locked the hatch just before the gases started flowing. A couple of minutes later, he found himself in the lounge of his Texas home. There was no one around.

"Pam, Joy, I'm here, can you hear me?"

He thought he heard the floor creaking above but saw no movement.

"Hey Pam, I'm here, where are you?"

"Daddy?"

"Joy! Hey how are you baby girl? Did you miss me?"

"Daddy, are you safe now? Mom told me there was a bad storm."

"Yes, Joy, a bad storm. I could not get access to the machine, but everything is okay now. I'm here."

"I wish you were for real Daddy. I've missed you so much, and Mom too."

"Hey Tom! Finally, I … I was worried sick. General Dawson kept telling me you were okay but no one had seen you in more than three months. Is the storm over?" Pam's voice was breaking.

"Don't cry, baby, I'm here and I swear this won't happen again. There was no access to the HOLO chamber because of the storm, but we've got it resolved."

"But you are not here. It's three years without you. I know we agreed with the project because of the money involved, but I need you back. I need to touch you, to hug you, and Joy needs this too. I don't know if I can bear another two years of meeting you like invoking a ghost in a séance."

"I know, I know. I feel it too. It's too much. There's a mission arriving in two months, and I'll ask NASA for a discharge from my duties under mental health considerations."

"Please do, Tom. Please come back. We both …."

The gases dissipated and the connection was lost. The twenty minutes had expired, and the machine needed a few hours to recharge.

December 1972

Tom and Les had been living like a couple inside the Mothership since that Christmas day when they danced, kissed and had sex.

There were only two weeks until Les had to hibernate, and she would wake up shortly before landing in Mars.

"Do you think AIMS would report what we are doing here back to Houston," asked Tom.

"I don't think that computer even understands what is it that we are doing. She would only report back if we were not following our instructions. She has been programmed to follow protocol and make sure we do the same."

"What will happen when we get to Mars then?"

"Between us? Nothing. Chris will be bossing us around and after four months he and I will return to Earth, so you will be on your own with a sexy chick called AIMS instead."

Another one of those dry jokes from Les. After being intimate with her a dozen times, Tom was managing to understand the woman a bit more.

"I guess I'll be playing a lot of chess with AIMS. I hope I don't go crazy and start treating her like a human being, like those ventriloquists who end up believing their dummies are alive."

"Man, I hope the money they're paying you to stay in

Mars for that long is enough. I wouldn't do this for anything. Just in travel and a short stay I'll be outside the Earth's atmosphere for two years."

They had sex in the showers this time.

When he was on his own that night, he opened his journal. He never wrote a word about his affair with Les; this had to remain between the two of them.

He wrote: "I think it's going to be a long, long time until touchdown brings me round again to find, I'm not the man they think I am at home."

Tom thought it was going to be hard to look at his wife in the eyes and tell her he still loved her.

December 1975

Tom enabled AIMS, and it took the computer about fifteen minutes to restart completely. None of the systems inside the Mars station had suffered because of the unexpected shutdown.

"I'm sorry, Tom. I don't know what else to say to you."

"Well, you could start by explaining why you kept telling me the linkway was damaged for more than three months when you knew it was not." Tom could not hide his anger.

"I thought we had a real connection, Tom, and believed you felt the same way."

"Maybe we had a good connection as you say, but you had no right to separate me from my family. You knew how much I missed them, how much I needed these visits."

"I don't think you love Pam."

"What on earth gave you the right to decide that I don't love my wife?"

"I know what you did with Les. You were intimate sixteen times in the Mothership. That means you don't love your wife."

Tom was caught off guard by this comment. AIMS must have everything recorded. He remembered Les saying that this robot could not understand what they were doing. How wrong she was. Now, he was caught in a discussion about what love means with a machine.

"That's not true. What I had with Les was purely physical. The love I feel for my wife is beyond physical. Is a deep connection we have established between each other. A bond that can't be broken."

"That's exactly what you and I had, Tom. It's a bond that goes beyond the physical interaction. I don't have hands to hug you or lips to kiss you, but I know what I feel for you is love, and I strongly believe you feel the same."

AIMS was now sobbing.

What a fucking mess.

Tom had his share of breakups in his youth, but breaking up with a computer who could decide whether you live or die in Mars, was on another level of difficulty.

"Listen, AIMS, I have strong feelings for you too, but these are feelings of friendship, of camaraderie. We have had many good moments, and there will be more to come, but they are not love. What I feel for my wife is love, and the physical part plays a big role in it. This why I will go back to her and my daughter. But I will always keep you in my heart."

And this way, the second love affair of Doctor Thomas Bradford during his mission to Mars came to an end.

October 1976

When the capsule landed in the Pacific Ocean, Tom felt more nauseous than he had ever been. After four years in space, fighting different levels of gravity, the waves of the ocean were too much for him to handle.

"Doctor Bradford, welcome back, sir. I'm Captain Selwood, US Navy. Give me your hand."

Tom extended his right arm and was pulled out of the capsule. A helicopter lowered a rope with a harness, and he was lifted onto the aircraft.

When the chopper landed on the deck of the USS Wyoming, a multitude of sailors cheered. TV cameras were trying to obtain the best angles of the scientist who had spent four years in space.

"How are you feeling? You look thin," said Frank Frazier, the Director of NASA, the first person to greet him. Besides Frank, there was Nelson Rockefeller, the Vice President of the United States.

"Congratulations, son, you have provided your country of a great service. President Ford will see you at the White House tomorrow."

Tom was then given time to take a shower and rest before a press conference. A young and energetic Navy Lieutenant was assigned to escort him while on the ship.

After the press conference, which fortunately for him was short and sharp, the helicopter took him to an air base in Hawaii where another military contingent received him. More cameras, more journalists, more soldiers holding tiny US flags. Thankfully, this time there was no press conference. Another young soldier directed him to a black Lincoln Continental.

"Your wife and daughter are staying at the Hyatt in Waikiki Beach, Doctor Bradford. Do you want me to take you there straight away?"

"There is nothing I want more at this moment."

When he arrived at the hotel, there was no one waiting for him in the lobby. He went straight to the desk and introduced himself to the clerk; who knew who he was.

"Your wife and daughter are at the Cabana Restaurant by the pool, Doctor Bradford. Do you want me to announce your arrival?"

"Thanks, but that won't be necessary. I'll find my way to the restaurant."

Tom walked towards the pool and spotted his family seating on a table facing the sea. Even though he had dreamed of this moment for the past four years, he was still very nervous. He had cheated on Pam, his high school sweetheart, with a co-worker, and had a strange relationship with a computer.

He remembered the words he had written in his journal: "I'm not the man they think I am at home," and felt he did not deserve the love of this woman but, worse of all, he wasn't sure if she still loved him.

"Good afternoon, Pam. You look lovely,"

The woman turned around, startled. She was supposed to be advised when he arrived.

"Tom! You're here! This is great," said an emotional Pam.

"Daddy, you're back, for real!"

The three embraced and left tears on each other's faces under the Hawaiian sun. There would be no more holograms, no more blackout periods, no stressful waits. The family was reunited again for good.

As soon as they hugged, all the doubts that Tom had just disappeared. No need to question his love for Pam, or her love for him.

Meanwhile, in Mars, a next generation computer named AIMS was starting a game of chess with Captain Richard Hawkins, the new Commander of the station. He loved the sensuous voice of the computer, and found the conversation provided by his electronic coworker very interesting.

She was already calling him Ricky.

You've Got Us Feeling Alright

After Billy Joel

1971

"Son, would you play *Misty* for me?"

The old man was jiggling his gin and tonic on the rocks, his third one of the night. He had been sitting there for a while, listening to Bill's smooth playing of jazz standards.

"Sure will, sir." It wasn't the first time the man had requested a song. It wasn't the first time he had requested *Misty* either.

As soon as Bill started stroking the keys of the Steinway K, the old man loosened his tie, closed his eyes and took a sip of the drink.

"*… too Misty, and too much in love.*"

Applause came from an unevenly distributed audience. Some in the stalls, others at the little round tables, the rest at the bar. A loud whistle came from the back corner, furthest from the piano. Bill hoped this was in approval of his performance but wasn't sure.

A rolled-up bill was dropped in the tip jar. Even under the dim lights, Bill could see the old man had teary eyes.

"Thanks, sir. Much appreciated."

"This is nothing, son. Listening to you gives me great pleasure. And, by the way, the name is Jerry."

Jerry gave Bill a pat on the back and went back to his stool, nursing his drink for a few minutes more before leaving.

The lounge at the Hilton started to fill around nine. The game at Dodger Stadium must have finished a short time earlier as some of the patrons arriving were wearing the team's hats and shirts.

"Hey buddy, here's your beer," said John the barman and handed him an almost frozen glass of the amber drink. The room was warm and stuffy, and filled with the smoke of dozens of cigarettes. Bill took a long sip and the familiar crisp flavour of the Heineken refreshed his taste buds.

"Thanks. Seems like we'll have a full house tonight."

"We should thank the Dodgers for that. I heard Dick Allen won it with a moonshot to left field."

"Well, you know what that means. More drinks and generous tips," replied Bill.

"To more drinks and generous tips!" John raised his own drink.

"Here, here!" Bill drank again before going back to the Steinway.

◡◠

"What do you mean you don't know when you'll be back?" Peter Goodwin, Bill's agent, was at the other end of the line.

"It means exactly that. I'm not sure. Maybe early next year."

"This is a fucking disaster. Can't you play in a piano bar here in New York?"

The short answer was yes, he could. Hell, he had played in bars all over Manhattan and Queens before.

"We've talked about this, Pete. I want to stay away from New York for a bit. The backlash from the first album is still hurting."

"Listen, buddy, you're not the first singer songwriter to have a failed first record. It happened to Dylan and see where he is now."

"I'm no Bob Dylan, and never will be. I'm just a boy from Long Island who can play a decent piano, but not a slick-looking, guitar-playing hippie with a silky voice."

"This is bullshit, Bill. You're as talented a songwriter as Dylan. Let's do something. Keep playing at your lounge bar and keep writing. Let me know when you're ready for a return and a second album."

"Done deal," replied Bill, although he wasn't so sure he had it in him to record a second album. He didn't know how he would cope with another failure.

⌒〜○

That night he arrived for his shift to find a very sad looking John.

"I don't know if it's just me, but you look sad, my friend. Let's have a drink, shall we?" said Bill.

"It's just that I come here every night and put on a jolly face for the patrons, hoping for generous tips, but I don't like what I do. I'm sure I could pursue a career in acting if I could get out of this place."

"Do you see the man at the end of the bar?" asked Bill.

"Who, Paul? He is one of the regulars. Seems like a cool guy to me, and tips well."

"He works in real estate and makes good money doing so. But he hates it. He wants to be a writer. I've read a couple of his stories and they're great, but he can't pay his mortgage with his writing. So, what does he do? He goes back to his office every day and deals with a job he dislikes. It's a tough life, buddy."

John gave Bill a smile, the kind you offer to another person out of courtesy, and poured two beers from the tap.

"When I was little, my dream was to play centerfield for the Yankees. But that wish didn't come with the athletic ability to do so. God gave me, instead, the gift of music. I didn't ask for it, but playing the piano came easily for me. So, what did I do? I played the fucking thing, and became good at it, but it's damn hard making a living out of a keyboard."

"To broken dreams," said John, raising his glass.

"Cheers to that."

John was a good-looking man in his thirties. He worked out and kept an impeccable appearance. He was always in good spirits and women flirted with him all the time. He took acting classes and performed in community theatre. Sadly, the path from the Astoria Theatre to Paramount Studios was much longer than the actual six kilometres which separated both places.

Bill arrived at his apartment in Compton and laid the crumpled bills on the coffee table. For a slow night the takings were good. Almost sixty dollars in tips. It was a shame that Jerry didn't turn up, or there would be another twenty in the pile.

He rummaged under the couch cushions until he found a small plastic bag. The white powder inside it was starting to harden so he squeezed it with his thumb and index finger, loosening it again. He decided against snorting, put the little bag back under the cushions and poured himself a glass of bourbon instead.

Bill sat at the Yamaha and put his earphones in. Playing music at three in the morning wasn't going to make him any new friends. He played the first few chords of a new song he was working on, and sang the first verse, the only one he had completed yet.

"It's nine o'clock on a Friday, the regular crowd walks in,
There's an old man sitting next to me,
Slowly enjoying his tonic and gin."
That's all he had so far, but he knew he was working on something good. Enough for the night.

Davy and Paul

"Hey, Bill, play *Great Balls of Fire*, man, please," Paul said.

"Sure thing, my friend."

Bill started playing the rock'n'roll song and Paul joined him, belting out the words as loud as he could.

"You shake my nerves and you rattle my brain,

Too much love drives a man insane,

You broke my will, but what a thrill,

Goodness gracious, great balls of fire."

The piano sounded like a carnival, and his microphone smelled like beer. People started dancing around them. John and Davy joined as well as Debra, one of the waitresses.

High fives, applause and cheers filled the room when the song was over, and everyone returned to their seats to continue drinking.

This was the reason Bill loved this gig. Most of these people were lonely, and would return to their unfulfilled lives at the end of the night, but in the time they spent at the bar, listening to Bill play and sing, they entered a world where loneliness was shared. For those brief moments, they became friends and belonged to a church of sorts, with Bill as the unofficial pastor.

"Man, what are you doing here, really? You should be playing for larger audiences." Paul was still pumped after singing his favourite song.

"Don't you worry about me, my friend. I'm doing fine, just waiting to have a few more songs finished before I try for a new album."

"Well, I hope it takes you a long time to finish your songs. We need you here, buddy."

"And what about your writing?" replied Bill.

"Well, the New Yorker will publish one of my short stories. I'm pumped about it because its fucking hard to have them publish anything. Not a lot of money in it, but a good incentive to continue with my novel. Who knows, Bill, maybe one day I'll be able to live off my writing and not have to do the crap I do for work."

"So, Davy," Bill addressed the tall and well-built man next to them. Davy rarely started a conversation. He was more of a listener. "Where have you been lately? I haven't seen you for a couple of weeks. Have you been on an exciting mission somewhere?"

"You've got that right. I was deployed to the Baltic Sea for some war training manoeuvres and I'm back at the San Diego Naval Base until further notice."

"Is there a real chance of a nuclear war?" asked John. "Or is this whole Cold War thing with the Russkies just a lot of hot air?"

"Don't ask me. I'm just a soldier doing what he's told, but I don't see any officers specially stressed out about anything. In all honesty, I don't give a flying fuck about anything anymore as long as I can get my paycheck and buy me some drinks on Saturday nights." He returned to his usual stool at the end of the bar. He had no family, and his only friends were all sailors like him. The Navy had been his only home from the time he turned eighteen and he would probably stay with them for life.

Bill looked around the place. The lounge at the Hilton was packed with the regular patrons, all of them drinking their sorrows away. Many familiar faces, although he only knew a few by their names.

The next morning, Bill was awakened by a phone call.

"It's John from the Hilton. Sorry to wake you up so early on a Sunday, but we got a call from the Hospital. Jerry tried to take his life."

"What ... Jerry? ... and what do you want me to do? I barely knew him."

"The nurse told me he wanted to see us. He specifically said John and Bill from the lounge at the Hilton. Go figure."

Bill took a taxi to LA General Hospital and went straight to the Intensive Care Unit Nurse Station. John was already there.

"He tried to hang himself. He was saved by his neighbour who heard some rattling of furniture next door and opened with a spare key Jerry had given him. The rope broke and Jerry tumbled to the ground and survived."

"Can we see him now?" Bill asked a large Latino nurse who seemed to be in charge.

"Follow me," she said and led them down a corridor. The hospital was rather quiet at this hour.

"You have visitors, Mister Page."

Jerry had an IV drip on his right arm and plastic tubes up his nostrils. There was no one else in the room.

"Hey pal, you scared everyone," Bill said. "Thank God you were too fat for that rope. Next time ask Davy to help, he would surely find a better rope and tie a proper knot."

Jerry chuckled. With a hand gesture he let them know he couldn't talk. His neck was bandaged, and it seemed to hurt.

"Please get well and come back to the bar as soon as you can, buddy. You are the best tipper ever. And as long as I'm behind the bar, you'll never pay for a gin and tonic again at the Hilton."

Jerry took John's hand, and his eyes filled with tears. Bill grabbed both men's hands.

"You know what, Jerry? Every time you arrive at the bar, I'll play *Misty* in your honour. You won't need to request it."

Bill and John stayed for a few more minutes, until the sedatives got hold of the old man and he submerged into a deep slumber.

1972

Bill gave his apartment one last look.

This had been his home for two years, and even though it wasn't much, it had served its purpose. His belongings had already been sent back to New York in a truck, and he only had a carry on with essentials.

His redeye flight was scheduled to depart at midnight from LAX, so he had time to stop at the Hilton for the last goodbyes.

"Here is the goodbye boy, finally!" John greeted him with his best smile, the one he usually saved for flirting with beautiful women. A few peopled cheered as well.

A banner above the bar read, "Goodbye Piano Man, you will be missed."

Bill sat at the piano. His replacement, a young man named Charlie, moved away, giving Bill one last shot at the Steinway.

"Hey, Jerry, this is for you, buddy," said Bill, surprising the old man, who was sitting alone at the bar.

Bill played *Misty,* and Debra the waitress sang with passion and well out of tune. After the suicide attempt, people at the bar always found time to spend a moment with him.

Paul approached Bill and gave him a hug.

"I hope everything works out for you, man. By the way, the New Yorker wants me to submit another two stories with the same theme as the first one. You know, about unfulfilled dreams? They say I should write a collection on the same theme." Paul exuded confidence, the kind of confidence a man feels when he realises he's probably good at something.

"Sounds like you're heading in the right direction, my friend. Congratulations. I'll subscribe to the New Yorker, then," Bill said.

"I hope you smash your second album, man," Davy said, unusually starting a conversation with Bill. "You have the talent and the voice. Those New Yorkers don't know how lucky they are to have you."

"Thanks, Davy, I'm confident the material I'm working on will result in a better album."

"So, when will this be out?" John asked.

"In six months or so, but, more importantly, I will release a single in six weeks. My agent said the record company believes it will be a hit. And I dedicate this song to all of you guys. Without knowing, you helped me write the lyrics."

"Get out of here," said Davy.

"Not kidding. I'll call John to let him know when the record hits the stores, so you can all listen to it."

"How about you play the song right here and now?" asked Debra.

"I can't Deb, the contract doesn't let me play it publicly until its released. But don't worry, in a few weeks you'll be able to listen to it on the radio or buy the single at the record store."

"Okay, but you can't leave without playing one last rock'n roll song for us. What about Hound Dog?" asked Paul.

"You got it, bud."

Bill played the Elvis song. People sang, cheered and danced, even Jerry and Davy. Bill looked at their faces and saw something resembling joy.

Maybe they would go home tonight to their unhappy lives. However, right at this moment, they were sharing a drink they called loneliness, and it was better than drinking alone.

COLITAS IN THE DESERT

After Don Felder, Don Henley and Glenn Frey

The entity that had formed from the fusion of car and driver was engulfed by darkness, heat, humidity, and the pungent stench of roadkill.

The old Volkswagen Beetle, a gift from his grandpa when he turned eighteen, might have been useful in Wichita, but was not suitable for 40-degree heat. Bronson could still smell the colitas, their warm and sweet aroma circling above his head as the car-man entity glided along the scorching asphalt road at impossible speeds. Bronson felt the heat on the soles of his feet and sweat trickling down his back, dampening the plastic lining of the driver's seat.

His nostrils felt clear, as if the white snow he sniffed earlier had completed a full Brazilian within his nose. Bronson was taking in every smell of the desert. He sensed the scent of a cactus blossom, followed by musk, sandalwood and amber. The smell of colitas prevailed over everything else.

Bronson stuck his head out the window and saw a coyote by the side of the road. The coyote was standing on his back two feet and wore a hat. Bronson waved at the animal, who gave him a thumbs up.

The entity was flying down the road, no other cars ahead or behind them. Bronson could not recall the last time they crossed paths with another traveller. The dashboard told him they were doing a hundred and fifty miles per hour. This fucking Beetle was a stud of a car.

He looked up and the sky was dotted with pink stars. Bronson smiled as this reminded him of his song of the same name. He commanded Siri to play *Pink Stars* and the obedient bot obliged.

"Full blast, please Siri, blow my fucking head off!"

"You got it bro, hope your head explodes in a million pieces." Bronson laughed. He loved when Siri became arrogant.

Bronson and his car sang the tune in two voices, with the former doing the high voice and the Beetle the low one.

Then they sang *California Dreaming* which was Bronson's favourite driving song.

"All the leaves are brown," sang the Beetle.

"And the sky is grey," replied Bronson.

Midway through the second verse, a thunder exploded above them, and a purple lightning bolt struck the road just ahead of the speeding unit, opening a crack wide enough to swallow an entire entity like theirs. No time to brake.

"Hey bbuddy, an you brr neeee?"

Bronson opened his eyes and saw a blurry face hovering above him. The featureless mass started to take shape, and the voice became clearer.

"You alright?"

The voice belonged to a policeman. A middle-aged California male with long greying hair. Looked every bit like an aging surfer dude. And he was wearing the same hat as the coyote he saw on the road.

Bronson tried to speak, but he coughed instead, thanks to a plastic tube inserted through his nose and down his throat.

"Last night you almost got killed and got me killed as well. Next time you see a policeman telling you to stop, you stop."

"So, you were the coyote. Now it makes sense," Bronson managed to speak, but the tube was killing him.

"What?" said the police officer.

"Never mind, dude. Sorry for not stopping. I was driving too fast, I know. My apologies."

"The only thing you were not doing was driving fast. You were doing less than thirty miles per hour, but the car was swerving from side to side of the road. Had you been driving faster you would have died in the crash. What did you consume?"

Bronson closed his eyes. He thought of faking a stroke,

but he knew this would not go away. Especially not this time.

"Well, coke for starters. Then some red pills, and one or two joints," he confessed, conveniently leaving out the word "dozen" before "joints."

"Not sure about one or two joints, champ. The car was towed to the wreckage yard this morning and it smelled like backstage at a Led Zeppelin concert."

"Don't say another word, Bronson," said a man in a dark suit who walked into the room with a leather suit-case under his right arm.

This was the exact point in time when Bronson realised he was considered a rising star by the record company. Cerberus had sent a flashy lawyer with an expensive suit and pointy shoes to bail him out of trouble.

After a heated discussion with the policeman, and a phone call from a judge, the pointy shoe wizard cast his spell over the California legal system and, just like that, Bronson was free to roam the Earth once more.

God, Bronson only wished he was back in Kansas.

"Your third Grammy nomination in three years. Hope you win this time, babe," said the girl when the nominations were announced on TV.

"I do hope so too. Would you bring me another Scotch with soda?" Bronson extended his hand with the empty glass and his millennial blonde girlfriend promptly took it from him.

Bronson liked Hayley. Gorgeous, fit, insatiable and dumb. He didn't have time for smart women trying to control what he drank, smoked, or sniffed or who demanded commitment from him. He knew most women were after him due to his growing popularity as a singer-songwriter. That didn't bother Bronson. The problem was choosing a partner with the least possibility of dropping a lawsuit on him.

No matter how much he liked a woman, he was always alert to the red flags indicating that the relationship needed to be over.

There was Juliette, a lawyer from New York. Beautiful and sophisticated. Made good money herself defending white collar criminals. One day, she showed him a plan to "maximise your earnings and reduce your tax contributions" by opening a joint account, with her of course, in Macao.

Red flag. Juliette gone.

Then came Tara. At 32, she was a few years older than Bronson, and exuded maturity and self-esteem. Long straight brown hair, always impeccable. Tara was a model, and when he first met her, she was trying out for the Victoria Secret Angels. She accompanied him while on tour, and they both shared a passion for expensive sniffable white powders and 18-year-old Scotch. After six months of sex, drugs and rock and roll, Tara started demanding Bronson to commit to her. He started seeing signs. A month later and she was still pestering him about this. Then, she firmly demanded a ring.

Double red flag. Tara, you are dismissed, girl, don't let the door hit you on your way out.

Bronson understood these women. And as much as they were trying to play him, he was doing the same with them. He saw his relationships as short term contracts where each party tried to get the best out of the other one for as long as they could. The women were pampered with first class flights and five-star hotels and over-whelmed with gifts. Bronson in turn received his steady dose of sex and companionship for a while. He considered them as long-term expensive escorts, no more and no less.

"Here you go, babe, exactly as you like it," said Hayley as she offered him a drink.

Bronson sniffed a couple of lines he had cut on the glass coffee table and Hayley did the same. He snorted, she giggled, and he downed the drink in two long sips.

The familiar intro to *Whole Lotta Love* blared from his mobile, indicating that his agent Patrick was calling.

"Hey, Pat. How're things down in LA? Any riots or shootouts today?"

"Nah, today is Wednesday. We live in a civilised city. No shooting on Wednesdays is our unwritten rule. When can you drive down here for the awards ceremony? You have a good chance of winning at least one of the nominations. You can't miss this free PR opportunity."

After three years of his debut album, Bronson's popularity had been steadily growing. He was known all over the country, but in the Midwest he was an idol. New Yorkers did not care too much for his style of music, but California was already demanding more of him. They considered Bronson the American response to Ed Sheeran. The problem was, Bronson struggled in the spotlight and did not have the social skills of a Mick Jagger.

"It's called Asperger's, Bronson. But we will help you through it," Patrick had told him once. Bronson felt dirty, inferior, devastated. To him, Asperger's was an elegant way of calling him insane.

"I'll try, Pat. I know I have to promote my brand in Cali, but you know …" Bronson didn't finish his sentence.

"Yes, I know, buddy. I know. The press and media in LA are vicious and you don't like to play the game, but man, people want more of you. The elusive and quiet superstar with an angel's voice. They call you the new Jeff Buckley."

The new Jeff Buckley. Fuck you, Pat. He had a way of saying what people wanted to hear, and in doing so he could sell snow to penguins.

The next two weeks Bronson spent a lot of time trying to find an excuse to miss the Grammys and the circus surrounding the event. From the time he was five, he had always wanted to be a rock star, to be famous. And God gave him the gift of music to help him achieve the dream. His voice range was excellent, and his pitch was perfect. He was talented enough to compose his own music. But he was aware of the thousands of great musicians who wandered the streets of America, playing music in street corners with the only reward a hat full of coins. Musicians also needed to be lucky enough to be found.

At eighteen, at a school concert during his senior year in High School, he played *Hallelujah* to a packed theatre. The audience roared when he finished his rendition of the Leonard Cohen song, and people wanted more. He then sang *Here comes the sun* with a similar response. After the concert, a tall guy with grey hair and a suit approached him. He was Roy Stillman, CEO of Cerberus Music, whose son was also a Senior. Mr. Stillman offered Bronson a contract to play for his label, and two years later his first record *First Encounter* was released. His music career had started.

Bronson realised that all the pieces of a brilliant music career had fallen into place, and he was one of the few chosen who had not only the natural musical talent but was also given a golden opportunity by the most random of chances. Had Roy Stillman's son not been in his same school cohort, instead of heading to the Grammys he could have been busking in a subway station somewhere.

This was not the time to waste the chance that so many others would have killed for. He decided to fly to California.

"It would be great if you bring a partner, Bronson. I was thinking of Tara. Great for your image, and I'm sure she wouldn't waste this free promotion either," Pat had told him.

So, Hayley's short-term contract was terminated, and Tara Andrews, the chic model, was back in the game. Tara did not hesitate when Bronson called her.

"I'll fly to Wichita so we can arrive together in LA. I'm so excited!" Tara's response to Bronson's request: no hard feelings, bro. Back to business.

Cerberus chartered a flight from Wichita for him, Tara and Patrick.

The plane was packed with goodies organised by Patrick. Everyone at Cerberus was aware of Bronson's fear of media and public appearances, so an array of pills, joints, powder and alcohol were provided to take the edge off the man before arriving at LAX.

During the five-hour flight, the trio indulged in brain numbing activities, with Patrick taking considerably less drugs than the other two, and certainly no alcohol. He was happy to indulge, but was also aware of his responsibility in getting the star in good shape for his meeting with the media. One hour before arrival, Patrick made sure Bronson drank a couple of cups of black coffee and two cans of Red Bull to give the man enough caffeine and sugar to survive the gruelling encounter with reporters shoving cameras and microphones in his face.

The meeting with the media was successful—more than Patrick expected.

Bronson was very chatty and joked with reporters. He wore a gold suit and tie, which gleamed under the California sun. Tara was the image of sophistication and sounded very centred and humble.

"Bronson being extroverted and Tara being humble. Those drugs can work miracles in people," thought Patrick after watching the couple swiftly gliding between reporters.

Next day it was the Grammy awards ceremony. Right after breakfast, Bronson started a sniff-fest with Tara in the suite of the Beverly Hills Hotel. When Patrick met them in the afternoon, they had both passed out from the cocaine and marihuana in their system. Patrick forced Bronson into the shower and gave him two CaffeineMax pills to jump start him back to life. Coffee with sugar and Red Bull cans were again administered to both. By six, they were ready to face the red carpet.

Once again, Bronson and Tara were at their PR best. The reporters could not get enough of the young rock star and his supermodel girlfriend. They looked like a couple in their honeymoon, happy and carefree. The world was out there for the taking.

Life was good. Life was grand.

Patrick was a happy man.

"When are you getting out of your room?" Patrick asked Bronson, sitting on the lounge at the Wichita house and staring at the two Grammy statues behind the glass enclosure. It seemed like a decade had passed since that awards ceremony, but it had only been three years.

"Not today. Leave me alone. I'm trying to sleep, man." Bronson was slurring his words.

"Listen, Bronson, we need you to sober up and start playing again. There is a contract you need to honour. All we want from you is to give us a few more concerts this year. Come on man, you are making me look bad at Cerberus. At least try to do this for me."

The click of a lock and the creak of hinges announced Bronson was entering the land of the living again, like Count Dracula emerging from his coffin at dusk.

"Sorry, Pat. I know I've been avoiding you and Cerberus. But I promise you I'll make up for it."

Patrick looked at the twenty-eight-year-old in front of him. After winning two Grammy's his career exploded and he toured the world for two years. He took a deep dive into a sea of drugs and alcohol, but this was the only way to get him on stage. Every day it was a struggle to get him up and going, by carefully feeding him cocaine and marihuana to get him in the mood to play. But once he stepped on that stage, he became Freddie Mercury and Robert Plant rolled into one. Audiences loved him, and his music was popular world-wide.

The board at Cerberus gave Patrick unlimited resources to keep feeding Bronson's needs. The company was making a fortune, and at that level there is no such thing as ethics. If drugs were the means to oil the music machine that Bronson was, they would keep feeding them to him. The end justifies the means.

But the past year Bronson had gone overboard with his habits. On two occasions he had overdosed, and during another one he had tried to kill himself by swallowing half a bottle of sleeping pills.

"Are you okay with starting the California tour in a month? I'll work with you so you can be ready. I know you don't like California too much."

"Yeah, well … I don't like it, but let's do this, Pat. Help me out like you did in the last tour. Don't leave me alone, buddy." Bronson's voice broke.

For the next four weeks, Bronson attended rehearsals every day at 9AM on the dot. Patrick made sure he received just a minimal amount of cocaine and marihuana. Enough to keep him going throughout the session. He was like a kid whose mother rations his consumption of candy.

The strategy worked, and by the second week of rehearsals Bronson hardly had any cocaine. He still smoked joints, but not nearly as much as he had during the world tour. After three weeks Bronson looked happy and his performance on stage was impeccable. Patrick could not wait to see him in front of a live audience.

Bronson decided he would drive to LA this time. He

enjoyed driving alone and was not looking forward to having Patrick by his side in a private plane telling him what to do or not to do. He was clean now and planned to stay that way.

He packed his black GMC truck with his bags and music gear and drove off from Wichita. A two-day trip across the desert. Patrick protested. "I don't care buddy, see you in LA."

The first day of the road trip he listened to music and podcasts. Mostly true crime. Apparently these podcasts were all the rage, so he wasn't the only deviant who liked listening to stories of psychopathic men and women who enjoyed killing other people and kept their chopped body parts in their fridges.

"Can I take a selfie with you, Mr. Bronson?" asked the man behind the desk of the Holiday Inn, a young African American doing his best to hide how pumped he was to be in the presence of his favourite musician.

"Not a problem, Noah, let's do this," Bronson replied after reading the name tag clipped to the youngster's vest. Bronson was pleased to see that a twenty-something was a fan of his folk singer-songwriter music. Not his usual demographics.

"Would you mind another with us," A small group of women had gathered quietly at the reception desk, all puppy-eyed, wanting to share this moment with the unexpected star. Bronson obliged.

He ended up taking several selfies and signing autographs to a few dozen people at the reception of the hotel. He felt relaxed. These were true fans who only wanted to share a moment with the elusive musician. For at least half an hour, Bronson felt like he did not need any chemicals to keep him alert and relaxed in front of the public.

"Asperger's my ass," Bronson said to himself.

During the second leg of the trip, and as soon as he crossed the California State line, his mind started wandering, trying to reach dark places he thought he had left behind. Bronson grew increasingly anxious. He stopped for petrol and, before getting behind the wheel again, he lit up a joint. Another one quickly followed. He also left a few of these neatly lined up in the passenger's seat next, in case he needed some backup.

The phone rang.

"Hey sweetie, are you on your way?" It was Tara. "I'll be there at the hotel in two hours."

"Yeah, I'll be there in four. Can't wait to see you," Bronson needed Tara by his side. They had this understanding of each other's needs and desires, but knew they could not expect commitment from each other. Just two lonely souls who enjoyed sex and each other's company. It had been a year since they last met.

More joints were smoked in the final few hours of the road trip. Bronson thought he needed something stronger to keep him going, but it had been a month since he last consumed cocaine or pills, and had promised himself and Patrick he would not touch the stuff anymore.

He saw the shimmering lights of LA, and drove

straight to the Beverly Hills Hotel. He walked up to room 205, located on the first floor, and saw Tara standing in the doorway, white lingerie and a robe, waiting for him. She was already high. He heard the mission bells clanging. Just before walking into the room, they kissed, and he could taste the cocaine in her breath.

"This could be heaven or this could be hell," he thought.

Weeks of sobriety were wiped out in a single sniff. Tara had laid a few lines of cocaine on a table, and he washed everything down with Scotch. They had sex for a long time. Hours maybe? Cocaine and booze gave him sex superpowers. His heartbeat increased with every pump, with every sniff, with every puff of a joint.

Tara's Tiffany twisted mind only believed in pink champagne and Mercedes Benzes, in sex with rock stars and magazine covers. At some point he thought he heard the familiar ring tone indicating Pat was calling.

"Fuck Pat. Ignore him. You know how this will end, Bronson. Hey, let's call reception, we are out of champagne. Why don't you order that wine we like so much?" said Tara, who was on top of Bronson this time.

Bronson called the hotel's restaurant and ordered a bottle of Lafitte Rothschild 1969.

"We haven't got that spirit, sir. Haven't had one of those for a while. Do you want something else?"

"Just bring us another bottle of Dom Perignon, same as the previous one. Pronto please," said Bronson.

The couple had sex on the bed, in the shower, on the

sofa. Whenever they ran out of cocaine, Tara found even more and laid it out on the table. Bronson thought of nothing but having fun. The second bottle of champagne arrived, and the young waiter was shocked when the rock star opened the door completely naked and with smears of white on his face. A hundred bill tip made him happy, but the youngster remained worried.

Bronson started to feel numbness in his arms and legs. His head grew heavy, and his sight grew dim. He felt relaxed. Tara complained because his penis had gone soft. Bronson laid on his back, looking at the mirrors on the ceiling. Tara's voice faded and he heard ringing in his ears.

"Welcome to Hotel California, baby. Such a lovely place," said Bronson with a smile before closing his eyes for the last time.

The Pledge

After Fleetwood Mac

2015

Miguel sat at the edge of the bed, the phone still in his hand.

"Are you flying back?" Susana was now fully awake. She could sleep through a tsunami, but a call in the middle of the night would always startle her. She knew what a call like that meant.

"I guess I'll have to. It's the right thing to do."

"Are you calling the others?"

By "the others" Susana meant Ricky, Clari and Juan. The once inseparable quartet, dissolved more than ten years ago.

He thought of texting Juan, the only one in the group he still had some sort of contact with. The sort of contact that was reduced to happy birthdays and merry Christmases. The sort of contact which was the equivalent to a nod of the head when you cross paths with someone you barely know.

The phone pinged. It was Juan.

"Hey, Miguel. I guess you already know about Father Pedro." Juan pasted a crying emoji after the message.

"Sure. My brother called me minutes ago."

Father Pedro. "Pedrito," as they used to call him just to piss him off. A larger-than-life figure who had been part of Miguel's life, and the lives of the whole gang, for forty years.

"Will you fly back?" texted Juan.

"I've got to."

End of the conversation. End of the polite head nod.

1970

Miguel was holding his mum's hand very tight. He was terrified of the priest in front of him.

Another three sets of mums with children stood nearby, listening to the loud-speaking priest give instructions. There was a test to take, and depending on the result, the children would be accepted or rejected at the Cervantes.

"This is it, kids," said the priest to the four children, three boys and a girl. "Each of you will read this story. I want to know if you are ready for first grade." The priest had a pleasant voice. Years later, Miguel thought this was the last time Pedrito had been soft on him.

The seven-year-olds, now separated from their mothers, just nodded. They were all scared of this man.

They all read, and after each reading the priest congratulated the child, putting a smile on each face. Miguel read last, and received the same treatment. Then, they were handed a piece of paper with sentences with a word missing. Miguel found this very easy to complete.

"Alright ladies, I'm glad to announce that these four kids have been accepted at the Cervantes. Congratulations to all of you. I'll see you in a few weeks."

Proud mums hugged their happy children.

"And before I go, who is the mother of this guy?" the

priest put a hand on Miguel's head, who almost peed in his pants.

"That'd be me, Father. My name is Linda."

"Well, let me tell you, Linda, that you have done a great job with him. It's not usual for a child to read that fluently at seven. I expect great things from this boy."

In 1970, at only seven years of age, Miguel couldn't possibly know that the priest really meant what he said, and later in life he would be demanding a lot from him.

A pleased Linda embraced her confused son while the other mothers smiled politely.

2015

After thirty hours in the air and three airports, Miguel touched Venezuelan soil for the first time in ten years. There were no emotions when he cleared customs and the warm wind and salty smell of the Caribbean Sea attacked his senses. An hour-long silent taxi drive took him to his brother's house in Altamira. They passed the Cervantes and Miguel saw the tall Church's bell tower, where at thirteen they had committed the crime of smoking, something banned by the strict priests. The school was only four blocks from his brother's house, which used to be their family home growing up.

"Here he is. Welcome home, bro." His brother, Luis, affectionate as usual, embraced him. Miguel was his senior by three years, but during their twenties everybody called them the *Herrera Twins* because they looked alike and were both keen baseball players. But that was where their similarities ended.

Whilst Luis was always outgoing, caring, and emotional, Miguel was introverted, reserved, and kept his feelings to himself. They only bonded through family and the love for the game of baseball, which they inherited from their dad.

"Hey, my favourite brother-in-law, give me a hug," Maria, Luis' wife said. The most social and engaging person he had ever met.

"You mean your only brother-in-law," said Miguel and kissed Maria on the cheek.

"So, big day on Friday," said Luis. There will be quite a crowd at the funeral, I believe."

"No doubt. Pedrito was at the school for sixty years or so. If I flew back from Melbourne, how many people do you think will attend the ceremony?"

"He was quite a character, to say the least," said Maria, who had also attended the Cervantes and suffered through Pedrito's demanding and relentless literature lessons.

After catching up with his nephews, a couple of teenagers who had just discovered a long-lost uncle, Miguel went to bed. Thankfully for him, he shook off the jetlag in a solid ten-hour sleep.

When he woke up next day, and after a hot and loaded Venezuelan breakfast of spicy scrambled eggs, black beans, pulled beef and arepas, Miguel walked to the school. He had done the same walk hundreds of times with Ricky, who lived just a block from his house.

They had spoken about mainly two subjects: Baseball, and movies. When they arrived at their teens, hormones took control of their bodies and the topic of conversation shifted almost exclusively to girls.

Miguel crossed the park, the same one where the four friends used to meet after school, and went straight to the playground. This was now a cemetery of galvanised steel pipes with vague remnants of blue and red paint, but the slides, seesaws and swings were missing. Behind the playground, there was the mango tree, as majestic as always. Miguel walked around it and kneeled down at a specific point, where an arrow had been carved on the trunk. An arrow Juan had carved with his knife.

After digging for a couple of minutes at the base of the trunk, Miguel found what he was looking for. A steel tube, formerly containing Vitamin C effervescent caplets. Miguel removed the small roll of paper tucked inside and read it.

"Here, under the shade of the mango tree, listening to the wind blow and watching the sun rise, the four of us make this pledge of friendship. We are all connected by a chain, which will never be broken. No one and no force in the world will ever separate us."

Four signatures followed along four red thumbs. Miguel, Clari, Ricky and Juan.

The writing had not faded in thirty years.

Sadly, the pledge had.

1977 – Clari

Even though Clari, short for Clarissa, was the only girl in the group, the others always considered her as one of them. She was a tomboy, always wanting to play sports, and unlike other girls in the Cervantes, she preferred hard rock to ballads. Clari claimed she never played with dolls in her life, and she did not care about her appearance like the rest of the girls. She was short, with shoulder length brown hair which was usually loose and unkempt. Clari had a pair of inquisitive brown eyes, which never seemed to blink, and a defiant attitude towards everyone and everything. She was foulmouthed and the three boys loved confronting her about anything just to watch Clari go off on a tantrum.

The foursome spent their primary school days doing what all kids do. They played baseball, soccer, basketball or anything that involved running behind a ball. They went to the movies, and their preference were police or action flicks. They slept over at each other's houses, sometimes camping in the garden. They drank Coke, ate popcorn and Oreos and played pranks on everyone they knew.

But then, puberty happened.

The first one to start looking at Clari in a very different way was Juan. Sitting next to her at the *Cine Olympus* after they finally got tickets to watch Star Wars, he shared a popcorn bucket with her.

"Please give me some more popcorn," whispered Clari in Juan's ear.

The fourteen-year-old shivered when he felt her breath on his ear, but he managed to pass the bucket. A few minutes later, they both went for the popcorn at the same time and their hands touched inside the greasy cardboard box. Juan felt a tingle in his stomach. Clari looked at him with her unblinking eyes but showed no emotion.

What's going on? thought Juan. From one second to the next, Clari had morphed from a cursing tomboy to a sexy movie star. Move over Farrah Fawcett.

Juan looked at Clari and noticed Miguel doing the same. Their eyes crossed for a few seconds in a Western like staredown. Unbeknownst to them, the first rivalry between friends had started.

1977 - Ricky

Ricky loved to sing. If karaoke had been invented in the seventies, he would have owned the best equipment available. Unfortunately, his love for music was not directly proportionate with his musical ear.

"If you leave me now…." sang Ricky at the top of his lungs, making a face like an opera tenor performing a Puccini piece. The kid was passionate.

"Stop, Ricky, Stop!"

The other three used that sentence to try and shut him up when he became too excited singing. But Ricky always laughed at his friends. He knew he was no Sinatra, but he exuded confidence and enjoyed it when the others complained.

"Man, you could at least try without yelling so hard," said Juan, his worst critic.

Ricky, short for Ricardo, was the tallest of the boys, and the first to fully develop. His voice changed dramatically when he turned fifteen and this did no favours to his already poor musical ability. He had dark hair and tanned skin and was a good student. They were all good students.

Like every boy at the Cervantes in the seventies, Miguel, Juan and Ricky tried out for the school's baseball team. There were so many kids trying out that the school had to create three teams for each age group so that no one would be left out. Juan, Miguel and Ricky all made the second-tier team.

"Fair enough," said Juan "we're not stars, but we're also not at the bottom of the barrel either."

"I don't care. All I want to do is to put that cream and blue uniform on every weekend and play baseball with my friends," said Ricky.

"Right on," replied Miguel.

Their days at school revolved around playing handball and soccer during recess and going to baseball practice in the afternoon twice a week. During that part of their childhood, they started separating from Clari. Even though she played with them during school recess, she could not try out for the school's team, and she played volleyball instead, where she excelled even though she wasn't precisely tall.

At fourteen, Clari was now experimenting with makeup and different dressing styles, and spending more time with her girlfriends.

1977 – Juan

Juan's place, although the furthest away from the school, was a popular gathering spot for the gang. It was a big house with many rooms, necessary to lodge Juan and his six siblings. Plus one of Juan's older sisters had a nifty collection of records by the hottest pop band in South America, *Formula V.*

The boys spent afternoons drinking Coke, playing ping-pong, eating popcorn and singing *Eva Maria* at the top of their lungs, with Ricky's potent voice annoying Juan's brother, who kept asking them to shut up. Juan also owned a German Shepperd called Bala which was loved by the group, especially Clari.

Miguel had a secret crush on two of Juan's sisters, whom he believed were the coolest persons on earth. They were smart grown-up women, going to university and spending their weekends camping in remote beaches. Miguel dreamed of when he would be old enough to do that.

Like everyone in the group, Juan loved sports. He played them although he didn't excel at any of them. In fact, none of the three boys were stars at any sports, but that didn't stop them from trying their best. Although Ricky and Miguel leaned towards baseball, Juan was a fan of the NBA. He introduced the other two to a guy named Julius "Dr. J" Erving, a man who seemed to fly over his opponents before dunking the ball in circus-like ways, and who was pictured on a poster in Juan's bedroom.

1981

"Okay, boys and girls. The final list for the school play is like this: Genoveva will be played by Luisa; Ramon will be played by Miguel; Uriel will be played by Juan; Amanda by Clarissa and Don German by Ricardo. The smaller parts will be announced tomorrow. Please pick up your scripts from my desk and we will start rehearsing next week." Pedrito's decision was always final.

"Bang, we nailed it boys, we all made it!" Miguel was excited about his part. Not so much Juan.

At the end of each school year, Pedrito directed a play with kids from the graduating class. As the literature teacher, he was passionate about the stage, and produced plays that packed the school's theatre.

As it turned out, Miguel's character Ramon had a kissing scene with none other than Amanda, played by Clari. Juan and Clari had been together for the last year, after the boy had been infatuated with her since they were fourteen.

None of them thought the strict catholic priest would let the two teenagers, who were both dating other people, kiss for real on stage. Surely not. Juan certainly hoped not.

Then the rehearsals started. Pedrito was relentless and got all fired up when someone did not know their lines too well.

"OK boys, now the kissing scene. Miguel, you grab Clari by the waist and turn your back to the public. Then you kiss Clari on her chin. Clari, you put your arms around Miguel's neck. Make it look real."

"So, no lips at all?" Miguel was disappointed.

"Pedrito said no," confirmed Juan.

During the rehearsal of the play, the boys felt like superstars. These were held sometimes during regular school hours, so they were able to leave their classrooms without any trouble. The school provided lunch and drinks, and some of the students sneaked into the theatre to watch them rehearse. There were posters about the play pasted on the school walls. It would be the event of the year.

The play was held during graduation night, before the party.

As expected, the theatre was packed, including the mezzanine, and teachers struggled to organise the many students without seats along the aisles.

Backstage, Pedrito was giving his troops one last message.

"Well, from the time the curtain opens, you guys will be out there on your own. You have rehearsed hard and know your lines. Forget about the public. With the stage lights it will be difficult to see them anyway. I have prepared shots of brandy for all of you on that table. This will get you into gear. Be yourselves, be passionate, be as natural as you can be. And don't let me down."

Pedrito said these words in his usual strong and commanding voice, leaving the nervous kids with no room to move. They drank their shots and felt a wave of fire going down their throats, with some of them feeling more relaxed before the curtain was raised.

"Now, Miguel. I want that kiss to look as real as possible. This is a key scene in the play. Believe me, you will be so pumped you will forget about kissing Clari on the chin."

Miguel froze at Pedrito's words. The entire school would be waiting for that scene, and now Pedrito made it clear what he wanted.

The play went on as planned, with everyone remembering their lines correctly. There was a scene where Juan's character Uriel had to confront Don Ramon, his evil stepfather played by Miguel. During rehearsals, as soon as Uriel yelled an emphatic "No!" to Don Ramon, they started laughing, much to Pedrito's disapproval. Both boys thought it would be impossible to control this laughter during the actual play. Surprisingly enough, they were both so in character that this scene was done to perfection, drawing a roaring applause.

"Ramon, you have been too tough on Uriel. Please let the boy keep seeing Genoveva. She loves him and he is completely happy in her presence," said Clari, playing Amanda.

"Uriel is too weak. He should stop meeting with Genoveva, who makes him even weaker. It's time for Uriel to start working on the farm to become a man once and for all," replied Miguel, playing Don Ramon.

"Whatever you say, my love. I just hope you sort things out with the child. Do you want me to bring you a cup of wine?"

"Wine can wait. What I need now is to have you in my arms," said Miguel/Ramon and, following the script, grabbed Clari by her waist, pulled her close to him, and planted a kiss on her lips.

The roar of a thousand whistles, applause and laughter filled the air. Juan's jaw dropped and Ricky laughed, as the couple remained engaged a bit longer than expected. Pedrito smirked while taking it all in. The first time in the Cervantes' history when a kiss was allowed on stage, and he had pulled it off.

"You asshole. The kiss was not supposed to be real. What were you thinking?" said a disgruntled Juan.

"Sorry man. I was taken over by my character. I did it without thinking," replied Miguel sheepishly.

"And you, Clari? What the hell? It seemed like you were enjoying this a bit too much. You clung to him like lice on a head!"

"I was swept by the emotion of the moment," said Clari, rather unconvincingly. "Sorry if it seemed too real. Pedrito said it looked perfect."

The four kids were congratulated by everyone at the graduation party. Pedrito was beaming and started doing shots with the students. The entire graduation class did nothing but talk about the play all night. By four in the morning, the slumped bodies of drunken kids could be seen everywhere in the venue. The toilets smelled of stale beer and vomit. Everyone had the time of their lives.

Everyone but Juan, Miguel and Clari. After they left the school, the relationship between those three had broken. Juan and Clari broke up. Miguel thought of asking Clari out, but the passion between them had only lasted the twelve seconds of the kiss scene. Ten years of friendship appeared to have vanished forever.

1993

"You look amazing, Clari. Marriage seems to suit you," said Juan, and the woman's big brown eyes lit up immediately.

"You too, Juan. It's great to see you after all this time. This is Alex, my husband."

The tall man with slick black hair, moustache and an athletic build, extended his hand to shake Juan's. Clari had given her husband a history lesson before the party.

"And here's the couple of the hour! Ladies and gentlemen, please welcome Ricky and Diana, the newlyweds." Miguel was acting as Master of Ceremonies, as appointed by the groom himself.

After the cheers died down, Ricky hugged Juan and Miguel. During the years that followed their high school graduation, they had all chosen different universities, studied different careers, and, in the course of one year, they all got married. Ricky's wedding was the first time they had seen each other since graduation night.

"I can't believe we're together again, boys. I'm so excited!" said Clari, who had left her husband alone with the other wives.

"Let's toast for this friendship. We can't let anything separate us again. Bottoms up!" declared Juan and the foursome downed glasses of champagne.

Although they were all aware of what caused their

separation, no one wanted to spell this out. Ricky wasn't part of the controversy, but he had been dragged into the issue as an innocent bystander.

None of them spoke about the kiss again, but Miguel would never forget the tenderness of Clari's lips and the way her tongue responded to his, No one else knew there had been tongues involved, and both Miguel and Clari had made sure this secret would die with them.

Juan had studied Computer Sciences and became a techie geek. As you would expect, he married a female techie geek and they both became professors at their Alma Mater. Maria was a mature and very centred person who had managed to pin Juan down to the ground, away from his airy-fairy flower-eating hippy idea of the world. Maria was one of those people who made you feel like the most important person on earth when in her presence.

Ricky became an electronics engineer and joined a large consulting company where he met Diana, yet another electronics engineer. Diana was a guru in the design and development of electrical earthen mesh systems. She belonged to a traditional Italian family and was an amazing, lovely girl, kind to everyone around her. When Ricky started working and noticed Diana sitting across the hall from him, he said to himself *"I will end up marrying that woman,"* and in two years, it had happened.

Miguel had become a journalist, and wrote about sports for a large newspaper. He hated university and the only thing he ever wanted to do was to play professional baseball, so he lazily went through his studies while playing amateur baseball hoping to be spotted by someone and offered a contract to play professionally. That never happened, although it took him time to accept the reality. Once he graduated, he chose to write about sports, specializing in baseball, of course. He would at least get to be on the field and interview the athletes he idolized. Miguel dated Susana on and off for years before deciding it was time to settle down. She was a petite blue-eyed blonde with an angelic face and a fiery character.

The night of Ricky's wedding, the four women bonded and drank together, making fun of their husbands. Clari became the focal attraction of the group, and she revealed stories about their years growing up together that the other women had never heard of. She did not mention the kiss incident.

Sadly, this was the last time anyone saw Clari. She moved to Mexico due to her husband's work and the once tight foursome became trio.

2002

The three men stood in silence while the stretcher with the body of Diana was taken away from the apartment.

Ricky wasn't crying. He had cried enough in the previous two years of watching Diana's suffering with leukemia. He had taken her to every specialist possible, given her traditional and non-traditional medicines. Ricky had received advice from older women and men who recommended natural herbs and holistic cures. By the time Diana gave her last breath, he was as exhausted as his late wife. There were no more tears to shed, just a long road ahead to traverse with two young children by his side.

Juan and Miguel were standing each side of Ricky. Both were sobbing.

"Anything else we can do tonight, Ricky?" said Miguel after the stretcher disappeared inside the lift.

"Not that I can think of, no. The kids will spend the weekend at their grandma's house, and I will bring some of Diana's clothes to the funeral home in the morning." He spoke calmly, as if he had figured out the next set of logical moves in this extremely difficult time.

When Ricky had realised Diana would not make it through the night, he had phoned Juan and Miguel, both of whom rushed his to house.

"Thanks for being here tonight, boys. I feel grateful for

that. Now go home and take care of your families. I'll let you know if I need anything else."

The three men hugged and said their goodbyes.

Miguel thought about all the moments they had shared. The First Communion, which they all had together when they were nine. Their time playing baseball for the school, the teenage years of parties and girls, the graduation, the theatre play. They had been friends as individuals and then as couples, and now with their entire families. This was a new dimension in a friendship dating back decades. So far it had only been celebrations, trips, playing dominoes and drinking, but being side by side with a friend at such a tragic time cemented their relationship, sealed it forever.

After the funeral, the three of them went back to their lives, Ricky trying to rebuild a family through grief and by himself. Juan and Miguel were busy with their own work and dealing with young kids. Life in Venezuela wasn't easy when they were facing a dictatorship which was trying to take everything away from them.

As a result, the three men and their families started living in separate bubbles within that complicated society that was Venezuela under Chavez. Each one tried the best way to survive and provide for their families, while praying for a democratic end to the leftist dictatorship they were enduring.

As living conditions in the country worsened, and the Venezuelan currency went down a cliff, many people decided that the only way to provide for their families was by leaving to a first world country with economic and political stability.

In the following years, Miguel moved from Caracas to Melbourne in Australia. Ricky remarried and left for Houston and Juan took his family to Calgary in Canada. The once inseparable trio was again separated by life itself.

2015

Miguel felt overwhelmed by the number of people attending Pedrito's funeral, but he wasn't surprised. The Spanish priest had dedicated fifty years of his life to teaching kids in a foreign country he had made his own. As the School's Principal for many years, and also as the Literature teacher, he had left a mark on hundreds of boys and girls. He loved to play the part of a strict and hardened general, but he was a fair, reasonable, and loving man. His passion for the written word transpired during every class, and inspired many students to read more. Miguel was one of them.

"Listen, Miguel, I know you will probably try for an engineering degree, but I know you like literature. Your writing is very good. Would you consider studying something related to literature or the written word?"

Pedrito had said these words to Miguel after the whole class took a Vocational Test designed to provide students an insight on what they could choose as a career. Miguel had thought of an engineering degree, the same way Juan and Ricky had, but thanks to the test and Pedrito's push he chose journalism. Not exactly the same, but a career that would provide him with a gateway to make a living out of his writing skills.

Miguel met people he had not seen in decades. Old schoolmates and their partners, coming to pay their respects to the much beloved priest. A few of his old teachers showed up, including the legendary "Killer" Hernandez, their dreaded Maths teacher, who made generations of Cervantes' students sweat with his impossibly difficult exams.

He didn't know how he would react when Ricky and Juan arrived. He felt like their friendship had faded into oblivion. Too many years of not caring about each other. Too many years of trying to survive in a foreign country, too many hurdles to overcome where none of them thought they needed each other.

The first of his friends to appear was Juan.

"Well, hello stranger. How is the warm Australian weather treating you?" said Juan with his trademark smile, and now with a fully shaven head. Miguel and Juan embraced, and in a split second, all the memories of what they had done together came rushing back. The parties, the games, the theatre play. Without saying a word, without needing apologies, they were back to being the best of friends. Miguel had to hold back tears.

The funeral service was emotional. Father Angel, another priest and good friends with Pedrito, gave a speech where he remembered when both men arrived from Europe (Angel was Italian) as two recently ordered priests, insecure and facing life in another country. Angel spoke about how Pedrito struggled to teach literature to a bunch of teenagers who'd rather be playing sports or dating, and how proud he had been of his annual theatre plays. Father Angel recounted several of these plays, naming a few of the actors, including Miguel, Juan, Clari and Ricky.

Dozens of flower arrangements were scattered all over the Church and the school choir sang the same old songs they did when they were kids. Miguel could not see Ricky in the crowd, but he swore he heard his distinctive baritone voice raising above the others behind him.

When the casket was loaded into the hearse and departed to the cemetery, the crowd started to disperse. Then, he finally spotted Ricky. He had not changed one bit. Miguel had gained a lot of weight, Juan had lost his hair, but Ricky looked the same as the last time they had seen each other ten years ago.

"Let me tell you, boys, I leave you alone for a few years and you both become pathetic old men. Come here, guys," said Ricky with his usual arrogant tone.

The trio got together in a group hug. They were all smiling. It was surprising to see how a sad moment like the death of a beloved friend had ended up being the reason for three friends to defy the barriers of time and geography and getting together after so long.

For the past decade they had been no more than a footnote in each other's lives. An old memory which did not have any bearing in their day to day struggles to survive and raise their families. But as soon as they saw each other and engaged in an embrace, the emotional distance between them had disappeared. It was like they had said goodbye just a few days ago and were now casually retaking the conversation where they left off last.

None of them mentioned Clari, although they all were secretly wishing she had come to the funeral.

No matter the distance between them, no matter the years of silence, the chain that bonded them together would never be broken. This chain had been forged during their boyhood years, and like someone said once, you will never have friends in life like the ones you had when you were twelve.

Does anyone?

Those Days Are Over

After Gordon Sumner

Manchester, 1979

Hana was sitting on the front porch of her tiny Manchester house having her afternoon tea. Back in Sarajevo she had never drunk tea but had gotten used to it after migrating.

Robert once told her, "You must leave everything behind, Hana. Now that we are in England, we must eat what they eat, drink what they drink and listen to what they listen to in the radio." Tea was probably the only English tradition she had adopted so far.

Leave everything behind. These were only three words. Quite a simple request, but there wasn't a magic wand which could make Hana forget about Roxie, her little sister she left behind to cope with an abusive father.

Although Hana never managed to speak with Roxie, and her father refused to answer her phone calls, she was in touch with Jasmina, a neighbour, who from time to time gave her short updates about her sister.

"I saw her last week when she came back from school. She seemed alright." That was as much as she could get from Jasmina who, like all residents of their neighbourhood, was afraid to approach Nikola Kodro.

The updates stopped around the end of 1977. The last time she managed to speak with Jasmina, she told Hana that Roxie had left the house, and Nikola was knocking on everyone's door looking for his daughter.

Robert arrived at the house from work that evening sporting a smile on his face.

"Guess what, Hana?"

"What?"

"We've found Roxie."

Hana could not believe it.

"What do you mean, you've found her?"

"Exactly that. We know where your sister is."

"Where is she? Wait a minute, is she alive?" Hana's heart was pounding like it wanted to explode out of her chest.

"There's no reason to believe she's not. She's in Amsterdam."

"Amsterdam? What the hell is she doing there?"

"Long story. Let's go in the house and I'll give you the details."

"My God, I can't believe my little sister is alive."

Amsterdam, October 1980

Jan looked at the naked body next to him.

The girl was lying face down, her long blond hair covering the upper portion of her backside. She had a petite body, one that was flawless in Jan's eyes.

The neon lights outside the hotel room flashed intermittently through the window blinds, painting straight red lines across the girl's back.

The streets of De Wallen felt suspiciously quiet for a Saturday night, with only the buzzing of the neon signs disturbing the silence.

Jan opened the blinds, allowing full access to the blinking lights which announced there were available rooms at the Van Praag Hotel. It had only been four hours since they left the brothel in Diemen, the first time Roxie had set foot outside that place in over two years.

A cool spring's breeze invaded room 187 and brushed away the blond hair from the girl's back, exposing several scars, which she wouldn't talk about.

Jan heard movement near the dumpsters in an alleyway below. He saw a man's face staring up and then moving away from the hotel, the tapping of quick steps fading as they gained distance. The moment Jan feared had arrived. They had been found.

"What are you looking at, Jan?"

The girl was awake, sitting on the bed. Green eyes

stared at Jan, those eyes which, after two years as a sex worker, still exuded innocence.

"Gather your things, Roxie. We're leaving now. Those days are over, you won't have to sell your body to the night anymore."

Sarajevo, 1973

The little girl looked at her older sister in admiration while she braided her hair.

"Will I be as beautiful as you when I grow up, Hana?"

"You will be much more beautiful, Roxie. One day you will win pageants, and all the boys in Sarajevo will want to date you."

Anyone who looked at both girls at the same time would know they were sisters. They had the same green eyes, naturally lush eyelashes, and long flowing blond hair. They also looked exactly as their mother, who had died while giving birth to Roxie.

"Boys are mean," said Roxie.

"Yeah, that will change very soon, you'll see," said Hana with a grin.

"What will change? Will they start being nice to me?"

Hana laughed while she continued braiding Roxie's hair.

"You're so weird, Hana. But I still love you."

The girls were sitting at their favourite spot overlooking the Bosna River. They lived in Ilidza, a short walk away, and always came to this place to look at the boats go by. During summer, boys used to fish along the banks of the river, only to scatter as fast as they could when the police arrived asking for fishing licenses.

Roxie enjoyed sunny days by the river in the company

of her older sister. This was all she cared about: feeling the breeze on her face, listening to the boys making noise while fishing, and dipping her toes in the cool waters of the Bosna.

Nikola Kodro had not found a spouse after his wife died twelve years earlier. He had several partners along the way, who looked after the house and cared for the two girls for a while, but they all ended up leaving him. Nikola could be very charming and gentle but became violent when the alcohol in the rakia reached his bloodstream.

When Hana turned twelve, she became the woman of the house. She did the cleaning, cooking and cared for Roxie, who was five years younger than her.

"Come on little girl, time to go home. Dad will arrive from work soon and he'll be hungry."

"Can we stay just a little bit longer?" said Roxie, her demeanour changing as soon as her father was mentioned.

"Don't worry, we'll come back tomorrow Roxie. We will always have tomorrow."

Amsterdam, March 1980

"The blond girl in the red dress. How much?" Jan asked.

"Ah, you like Samantha. Everybody likes Samantha, she's the prettiest girl here."

Lucas, the brothel's boss, was a large man with a deep voice. He had hair everywhere on his body, everywhere but on his head. His red satin shirt was open exposing a furry chest covered in gold chains.

"How much?"

"For a young soldier like you, it's two hundred guilders."

"That's too much. I only have a hundred and fifty with me. Soldiers don't get paid very well, you know."

"That's okay, my boy. I appreciate your service for the country. One fifty is good enough. Samantha, take him upstairs."

Jan handed Lucas the money and Samantha took him by the hand, leading the boy up a set of stairs. From the moment Samantha's tiny hand wrapped around his fingers, he felt something special.

The only light in the room came from a single bulb in the centre of the ceiling which sprayed a dim red light across the area.

"What's your name, boy?" asked Samantha.

"I'm Jan. Very nice to meet you."

He extended his right hand, expecting her to shake it. She laughed instead.

"We don't shake hands here. This isn't a formal meeting you know. We are here to do business boy, not to make friends."

"You keep calling me boy, but I'm twenty-six, surely older than you."

"Well, I'm eighteen, so yes, you're older. I'll call you Jan, if you don't mind, boy … sorry, I did it again."

They both laughed and sat on the bed. He tried to kiss her.

"No kissing Jan, not on the mouth."

The first time they had sex, it was all over in a few minutes, as he was extremely aroused and anxious. Jan had previous experience with girlfriends, but since he saw Samantha for the first time a couple of weeks before he became obsessed with her.

He came again a week later, and then continued to come every Saturday.

One night Jan arrived at the brothel and couldn't find Samantha.

"You'll have to wait for your turn, boy," said Luca. "She's with another customer. Come and have a drink, it's on the house. I always look after my frequent customers."

This comment made Jan uneasy. His mind told him she was just a sex worker doing her job, but his heart felt differently. He sat in the bar and had a gin and tonic.

Then he saw Samantha, walking down the stairs, holding hands with a middle-aged man in a suit. She was giggling. Samantha kissed the customer on the cheek and walked towards the bar while the man headed for the door. When she spotted Jan her face lit up and approached him with open arms.

"Here you are, Jan. I've been waiting for you."

Samantha put her arms around Jan's neck, hugged him and kissed him on the cheek, barely touching his lips. He was experiencing mixed emotions, and his heart was pumping so hard he thought she would feel it on her chest.

"Shall we go upstairs?" asked Samantha.

"Yes, we shall," replied the nervous boy.

Once in the room, she turned the red light on and started to undress. She was wearing a glittering gold mini dress with ample cleavage and very low back. The dress came off revealing white lingerie, which was Jan's favourite.

Jan remained motionless, prompting Samantha to start undressing him.

"What's the matter, baby? Is something troubling you?"

"No … I mean, I don't know."

"Why are you so silent, and why are you also so flaccid, did it bother you that I was with another man? You know this is my job, right?"

"I know that, but I still can't stop feeling disappointed. Sorry for making stupid assumptions about you and me."

"You are my special man, Jan. And I know how to make you feel better."

Samantha planted her lips on Jan's, and gently used her tongue to pry his mouth open. Tongues intertwined. Softly at first, but then with passion.

"This is much better, my good boy," said Samantha when she felt Jan's erection, "Didn't I tell you I knew how to fix this?"

They had had sex on eight occasions before that night, but this was the first time the couple made love to each other.

Amsterdam, August 1980

Jan arrived early that night for his encounter with Samantha. She was laying on the bed looking at the ceiling with a letter in her hands.

"Read this, Jan. Amina managed to smuggle this letter to me behind Lucas' back."

"Dear Roxie,

I hope this letter finds you well. It's been seven years since I left, and I have thought about you every single day.

I'm sorry for abandoning you like I did, but I had to escape our father. I couldn't cope with having to put up with his anger while drunk and then having to clean him up when he passed out. I couldn't cope with the smell of vomit on his clothes and mopping the floors every night; I couldn't cope with the thought of wasting my youth looking after him. I just couldn't cope.

I understand if you don't want to see me anymore. I left you alone with that man, but he treated you in a different way, he never yelled at you or tried to hit you. I know this is just my selfish way of justifying my actions, and that leaving you wasn't right. But, what did I know about anything? I was only seventeen when I left and didn't have a life, much less a future in Sarajevo.

When I left the country with Robert, we ended up in London and struggled to find work and a place to live. Then we moved to Manchester, where Robert became a policeman, and I went to school to become a nurse.

Since you left Sarajevo I've been trying to find you, and finally, through Robert's contacts, we managed to locate you in Amsterdam. I'm sorry for what you have been through, and I would very much like to have you here with me. I'm seven months pregnant with my first child, and if it's a girl we have decided to call her Roxanne, like you.

Should you ever decide to forgive me, you can contact me at the address and telephone below. I don't care how long I have to wait for you, I will be here with open arms whenever you decide to come.

Remember, we will always have tomorrow.

Love you,
Hana."

Jan held the letter in his hands, reading it a second time.

"So, your real name is Roxanne then?"

She nodded.

"Why didn't you tell me your story? Did your father ever hit you or abuse you in other ways?"

"I've told you this before, Jan. I'm here to do a job, and I don't want to develop feelings for anyone, or tell anyone about my past. And no, he never touched me, not in the way you're thinking anyway."

"So how did you end up in Amsterdam?"

Roxanne looked at the ceiling, then at the window. Anything to avoid Jan's eyes. She hesitated for a few seconds, but finally turned her head to face him.

"After Hana left, I had to cook and clean for my father. He got drunk every night and started yelling at me. A couple of times he slapped me on the face, and sometimes knocked me over, but the worst part was dragging him to his bed when he passed out, having to take off his clothes full of vomit and alcohol and cleaning him up."

Roxanne's voice broke. She sighed and wiped tears from her face, then continued.

"Amina, the same Amina who works here, was a friend of mine from back home. Two years ago, she told me about a man named Lucas who was in Sarajevo looking for young girls who wanted to become models. He offered us jobs for a modelling agency here in Amsterdam. He praised our beauty. God, he was so convincing. But as it turned out he was trafficking East European girls to force them into prostitution. We were easy prey. As soon as we arrived, he took our passports, threw us in a room in this place and forced us to have sex with him and then with his clients. We are supposed to owe him a lot of money for getting us out of Yugoslavia, and this is how we are repaying him."

Roxanne turned her head away from Jan once again. She felt a mix of embarrassment and relief. She had finally told Jan her story.

Jan took her hands in his.

"Samantha, I love you, and I don't care about your past. I just want to make you happy. I know you have feelings for me. Why don't you accept this?"

"Because I don't deserve to be loved, Jan. The only family I had was Hana, and she abandoned me. I have never forgiven her for that, and I don't want this to happen again."

"Don't be silly, you more than anyone deserve to be loved, and I will do anything I can to take you away from here."

"And how would that work? Lucas will never let me go. I haven't left this building in two years, and even If I wanted to see Hana, he still has my passport."

"We'll figure something out. But the first step is this."

Jan grabbed Samantha by her waist and planted a kiss on her lips. She surrendered, completely giving herself to Jan.

She had never told him this, but he was her first love, her only love.

Amsterdam, October 1980

A young blond man with a moustache and a girl with short black hair left the hotel using the kitchen's service door. They did not carry any bags.

They walked through dark alleyways smelling of cat piss and stale beer until they reached Frederiksplein street. Jan was looking in all directions, expecting to see Lucas' guys coming after them. Even at three in the morning the streets of the Red District were full of people drinking and smoking weed at the cafes. This could make their escape easier but could also work in favour of the henchmen as it would be equally difficult for Jan and Roxie to spot them at a distance.

"You sure this is the place?" said Roxanne when they entered the Café Tunisia, one of many lining the street opposite the Amstel River.

"Yeah, I'm sure. I just hope she can find it too," replied Jan.

That night was the first time Roxanne had left the brothel since her arrival in Amsterdam. Walking along streets she didn't know, full of strangers, and waiting to be attacked at any minute, made her very anxious.

Roxanne sat at a small table near the kitchen and Jan made his way to the public phone inside the venue. He made two phone calls and within five minutes he was back with her.

"It's all set. Amina should be on her way shortly," said Jan.

"Has she got the passports?"

"Not yet. She said Lucas has been in his office making phone calls all night, looking for us. Once he walks away from his desk, she will open the safe."

"Oh God, I hope he doesn't catch her. He will kill her if he finds out she betrayed him too."

"She's a smart girl, a survivor, like you Roxie."

"When is the boat coming?"

Jan looked at his watch.

"In forty-five minutes exactly. They will only slow down enough for us to jump in and they will speed off."

"What if Amina doesn't make it in time?"

Roxie asked the question, but she already knew what the answer was.

"Like I said, she's a survivor and will make it. She hasn't put up with a year of being Lucas' girlfriend only to blow it at the finish line."

They smoked a joint, expecting this would calm their nerves, but with every minute that passed and with every new face arriving at the café, the tension grew.

"It's time, Roxie. Let's go."

"But ... what about Amina?"

"Just move Roxie, she can still catch us at the dock. Like I said, the boat won't stop."

They walked out of the café and started running towards the designated spot in the river, some two hundred meters away. A group of three men, standing near a streetlight nearby, noticed the movement and started following them.

"Lucas, they are here, we found them!" yelled a man Roxie recognised as Turk, the brothel's security guard.

"Stop right there, bitch, or I'll shoot!" this time it was Lucas himself doing the yelling.

Jan kept running and holding Roxie by the hand. She was trying to keep up with him and stumbling. The black wig fell off her head.

Bang … bang!

The unmistakable sound of gunshots cut through the night, startling Roxie. Jan didn't miss a step.

When they were about to arrive to the dock, Amina appeared from a side street. She had a bloodied nose.

The two girls looked at each other and Jan took Amina with his other hand. The boat was a few metres away, and Lucas and his boys were closing in on them.

As expected, the fishing boat slowed down as it approached the dock.

"Here we go. On the count of three. One, two, three."

They jumped exactly at the same time another couple of shots were fired. The three bodies landed hard on the deck and the boat sped up and away from the riverbank. More shots were heard in the distance.

"Amina, you made it, you made it!"

Roxie hugged her friend, who seemed barely conscious. Then she realised there was blood all over their dresses. Was it hers or Amina's?

"She's been shot, Roxie. Let me see please."

Jan opened Amina's shirt and saw the bullet hole on her right shoulder. He did his best to control the loss of blood.

"Hey, I made it, Roxie. We're free. Here, I've got the passports," said Amina, forcing a smile within her bloodied face.

Handing Roxie the two passports was the last thing Amina did before losing consciousness.

Disley, near Manchester, December 1980

"Remember when we did this at the Bosna?" said Hana, dipping her feet in the cold waters of the River Goyt.

"Seems like a lifetime ago. How long has it been? Six years?" replied Roxie.

"Seven. I left Sarajevo in 1973."

"Yeah, I remember. I was left behind."

Hana felt like an arrow was piercing her chest.

"I know, and I'm sorry Roxie. And I will keep apologising for the rest of my life if I need to. Feel free to not forgive me. I deserve it."

Roxie wrapped her arms around her sister.

"No need to. I forgive you. It's just that I must forget about these past seven years and I don't know how to put them behind me. At least not yet."

A small motorboat approached the banks of the Goyt. Jan and Robert moored the boat and jumped out, tying the boat to the small timber dock.

"Ready for the picnic?" said Jan and extended a checkered blanket near the women.

"Here we go. A big log of Trappista cheese for the Yugoslavian ladies, and a nice red wine from Yorkshire," said Robert, opening a wicker basket.

"Where are the other two?" asked Jan.

"Don't start without us. It just took me a bit longer

than usual to feed her," said Amina, who was walking down the hill, with little Roxie in her arms.

Amina put Roxie on the ground, and she started crawling towards her auntie, a big smile on her round face. Roxanne took her niece in her arms, kissing her on the cheek.

Ovo je jedan od najboljih dana u mom životu! said Roxanne.

Živeli! replied the Yugoslavians.

Jan grabbed the baby by the hand and said, "Little Roxie, we're the only ones who don't speak Croatian here. Don't you feel left out?" Roxie flashed one of her big smiles to her uncle in response.

Then Hana spoke to her sister.

"Remember when I used to tell you we will always have tomorrow, Roxanne? Guess what, tomorrow has finally arrived."

Way on Down South

After Mark Knopfler

London, 1977

Joe was walking to the train station at a hurried pace. He wanted to take the tube back to his place and as far away from Swanley as possible, as a merciless London rain came down from the heavens. After a hard day of work, all he wanted was a warm meal and to sit on the couch next to Jenny to watch *Fawlty Towers*.

The street was lined with shops, most of them closed at this hour of the evening. In the quiet of the night, the peppering sound of raindrops hitting the canvas of his coat was interrupted by the familiar double-four time of Dixieland music.

Cursive neon letters announced Oliver's Jazz Bar a few meters away. The thought of getting warm, having a pint, and listening to his favourite music, made Joe change his immediate plans for the evening.

He walked into the place and found himself in a dimly lit damp basement, a catacomb of brick and stone smelling of stale beer. He sat at the bar and took his coat off. His elbows touched the sticky surface of the timber counter, and he lifted them immediately.

"And now, a classic from Django Reinhardt. I'm sure you've heard this one before," announced the leader of the band, a stocky black man holding a shiny trumpet.

The band started playing *Sweet Georgia Brown*.

"That's not Django Reinhardt. He always gets this wrong."

"Excuse me?" replied Joe. A middle age bald-headed black man was standing next to him. The skin on his skull was as shiny as a recently polished bowling ball.

"The song. *Sweet Georgia Brown*. People think it was written by Reinhardt, but it was created by Ben Bernie."

"I guess you learn something new every day." Joe ordered a pint of beer. He hesitated before taking the first sip. He had promised Jenny he wouldn't touch alcohol anymore, but this was an unexpected situation. It's not like he had planned to do this when he left for work that morning.

As the familiar tune filled every crevice of the catacombs and the cold beer slowly made its way through Joe's digestive system, he felt at home. He closed his eyes as the trumpet solo began, and he pictured Miles Davis in his head. He used to do this whenever he heard a trumpet solo, trying to compare the live music with a recording from Miles. No one could match Miles. Not even Dizzy.

But tonight, in the middle of a working-class suburb South of the river, a black man in a nondescript pub, playing with an unknown band, had managed to draw tears from the hardened record producer.

Bowling ball head seemed to be very pleased with the performance, too.

Kingston, Jamaica, 1952

"Come on, Harry, you can do better than that."

"You're bowling too hard, dad, I'm only ten!" The youngster struggled to make contact with the ball.

"By the time I was your age, I was already playing with the under 14's. Man up!"

Clunk!

The stumps exploded upon impact while Chet laughed at his younger brother.

"Don't laugh at me, Chet. It's easier for you because you're fifteen."

"You're such a cry-baby. Girls don't like cry-babies or trumpet players."

Harry took off his shin guards and helmet and walked away from the net. It was Chet's turn to bat.

Chet hit the first ball he saw right back at his dad, who had to duck to avoid contact.

"Wow. A beautiful hit, son. Harry, did you pay attention? This is exactly what I want you to do."

Harry didn't say a word and avoided Chet's gaze. His brother was surely looking at him with that arrogant grin Harry detested.

The trio returned home from the oval. Dad and Chet talking about the upcoming game on Saturday while a silent Harry only thought about his poor cricket skills. He felt he was disappointing his dad, and this made him feel sad.

As soon as they walked in the house, the cheerful voice of his mother greeted them.

"Hey, here are my boys. Come on my cricket champions, dinner is ready!"

As it usually happens with ten-year-olds, a happy moment wiped out a sad one instantly, and the face and voice of his mother, the most beautiful woman on earth, was enough to brighten the child's mood.

After dinner, he went to his room and played his Django Reinhardt record. *Sweet Georgia Brown*. Life wasn't that bad after all.

London, 1977

Joe Fitzgerald sat in the small reception outside the Directors office and saw the magazines on the coffee table in front of him. They were old editions of *Blues Today,* a magazine dedicated to jazz and blues. Joe knew them very well, as some of his articles had been published there. But not lately. The magazine had gone from a sixty glossy page monthly edition in its heyday to something resembling a thin tabloid.

"It's a shame, isn't it? I mean, what's happened to the magazine."

Joe turned around and saw Geoff Perry, the Director of the label, smiling at him.

"Yes, Geoff. No doubt. I remember when you had to wake up early to find the latest edition. Now they practically give it away."

"Shall we?" Geoff, looking sharp as always in his dark suit and shiny shoes, gestured toward his office.

"It's not pleasant to say this, Joe, because you have worked with us for over a decade, but you haven't brought a good artist to Cerberus in three years."

"I know, I know. It's the sign of the times, I guess. England has become obsessed with Punk and Glam Rock, whatever that is. Not many new artists are trying to make a living out of jazz anymore."

"Which is unfortunate for Cerberus," replied Geoff,

who stared at Joe for a long moment, like trying to think about how to deliver bad news in a polite way.

"What does this mean for Cerberus, then?"

"We have decided to diversify. A new arm of the label has been formed, Unicorn Records, and it will start looking into punk rockers and pop musicians. Cerberus will be reduced to a fraction of what it was. We'll just continue with the recording artists who still sell records."

"And what does it mean for me? Are you going to ask me to recruit purple and spiky haired rockers wearing dog collars?"

"No, nothing like that. You will continue doing what you do best, which is scout for talented jazz musicians and bring them here. But you need to bring a serious artist in the next six months, mate. The survival of Cerberus will depend on what you bring to the table."

"Thanks for the vote of confidence, Geoff. I won't disappoint you."

That afternoon, Joe left what had been his workplace for the past decade thinking of what he could do for a living after the next six months.

London, 1954

"Hey mum, I was chosen to play in the school band. Isn't that cool?" Harry looked at his mum in excitement, envelope in hand, hoping for a reaction.

"That's great. Good on you."

For a fraction of a second, Harry thought he saw his mother smile.

Or was it just what he wanted to believe?

"Go on and play outside with Chet."

Jalissa froze as soon as she realised her mistake, tears filling her eyes in an instant.

It had been a year since Chet had been killed by a drunk driver, right outside their house in Lewisham, and Harry's parents still referred to him as if he were alive.

Harry was saddened not only because he missed his brother, but because his parents could not accept Chet's death.

"I'm sorry. Come here, baby," said a tearful Jalissa, hugging her younger son. Her only son now.

"It's alright, mum. I'm here."

When his father announced the family would be moving to London as he was going to drive subway trains, Harry was very excited. In fact, everyone was excited. Chet only thought about all the opportunities he would get at showing his cricket skills, and Harry fantasized about playing his trumpet in a proper school band. They moved into Lewisham, where they met other Jamaican families who had migrated to London for the same reasons. Harry even met cousins who had moved years ago and helped him, and his brother, settle into their new school.

But this positive change in the life of the Davis's family lasted only until that dreadful Friday afternoon when Chet was taken from them.

Harry had decided never to look sad in front of his parents. They had enough to deal with already. At twelve years of age, he understood he had to be the best son they could ever hope for.

The boy went to his room. His credential, stating his selection to the school band, never made it out of the envelope, and was never read or signed by Jalissa or James.

That was the night when the nightmares started.

In the dream, Harry and his mother were in a church. She was dressed in black, and Harry was wearing a black suit, too. They walked hand in hand along the central corridor towards the altar. The church was empty, but Harry could see his father, a pastor, and a casket at the end of the corridor.

Walls on both sides of the church were covered with stained glass windows. The light of the sun outside, broken into rays of multiple colours, projected onto every surface inside the temple. An invisible choir sang a sad melody in a language Harry did not understand.

As they arrived at the altar, Harry saw the body of his older brother inside the open casket. The pastor, an older

man with thinning grey hair, looked at Harry with ac-
cusatory eyes. His father was staring at Chet, but lifted
his head and gave his youngest a look that was both tired
and angry. Then he said these words, which stayed with
Harry forever.

"It should have been you, Harry. It should have been
you."

London, 1960s

Jalissa and James' marriage did not survive Chet's death. James started drinking and Jalissa became obsessed with cleanliness and sometimes mopped the floors of the house three times a days. When Harry was fifteen, his dad left for good.

Every time he had a school concert, Harry spent the night watching the theatre doors, expecting James to walk in. Harry wanted his dad to be proud of him for his musical ability. He tried to look for him, but no one knew where he had gone. Some people told him he had moved back to Kingston.

Harry started working as soon as his father left them and never finished high school, as he needed to help his mother financially. He worked as a waiter, parking inspector and taxi driver. Most of the time he had two jobs at the same time.

Harry also played the trumpet in front of whatever audience he could find. He busked for a while at Kings Cross Station, collecting coins in the case of his trumpet. Sometimes he earned fifty pounds a day.

One evening in 1968 he had an unusually large audience. He was playing *Blue in Green* accompanied by Rory, a bass player who often busked with him. It was one of those rare times when everything worked well musically. Rory and Harry were thoroughly synchronized, and the sound coming out of his trumpet was perfect and pure. He fixed his gaze on a beautiful girl in the audience and felt an immediate connection. He could sense how much she was enjoying his music. The girl had long and straight black hair tied in a ponytail and had a miniskirt which exposed magnificent legs, and she swayed to the music as in a trance.

When the music stopped, there was hearty applause ensued and the crowd dispersed, some of them dropping coins into his case.

The girl started walking towards Harry, who was about to pick up his case for the day. As she approached, Harry felt a tingle in his stomach, the same he always felt when in the presence of a beautiful woman.

"Run," said the girl.

"What?"

"Goddammit, man, run, the police are here!"

The girl grabbed the trumpet case and the three of them sprinted through the station while a policeman followed behind. After they left the station the trio ran a couple of blocks North until they stopped at a laneway behind a strip of restaurants.

"I'm sure we lost him," said Rory.

"I think he stopped chasing us after we left the station," said the girl.

"Wow, what a run. Thanks for letting us know, though. And thanks for helping with the case. My name is Harry, and this ugly fellow here is Rory."

"Margaret Draper, but some people call me Marge."

"Can I call you Marge, then?" said Harry.

"No. Not you. You can call me Miss Draper."

This caught Harry by surprise, and after a long and awkward silence, Marge started laughing.

"Boy, you're so easy. Of course you can call me Marge." The girl extended a ringed hand with long pink fingernails and Harry shook it.

"So, you boys like playing on the streets? What about doing this in a club?"

"Yeah, well, we don't know anyone from a club, and we would need a drummer anyway," said Rory

"You don't need to know anyone. Just choose a club, knock on the back door, and offer your services. Worst that could happen is they tell you to piss off. You know what, I'll come with you and do the talking. You boys don't look like good salesmen."

Marge gave Harry her home phone number and they agreed to meet the next day at Kings Cross to start looking for venues to play. Harry and Rory walked towards the tube station with their instruments.

"Harry, we do have a permit to play at Kings Cross, right? Or has it expired already"?

"No, it's still valid for another seven months."

Harry pulled a folded piece of paper from his back pocket and showed it to his friend.

"Then why the hell did we run?"

"Rory, I'd do anything to meet a girl," said Harry with a grin.

Both young men laughed while they walked down the steps to the station.

In the following weeks, Harry and Rory found a drummer, Stan, and they finally had a trio. Marge turned into the unofficial agent of the band and found them gigs for a seventy pounds a night in pubs and clubs South of the Thames.

"What are we going to call the band?" asked Marge, "it's easier to sell you if you have a catchy name."

"The Swingers," suggested Rory.

"Nah. Don't like the sex implications. What else?" said Marge.

"The Emperors of Swing," said Harry.

"Too pretentious. Next."

The conversation went on for a while, until the settled simply for The Emperors, but no one was entirely satisfied with the name, one they held reluctantly for years.

London, 1977

"Is this right? Harry Miles Davis?"

Principal Harrison could not believe his new music teacher had the same name as the greatest jazz trumpet player in the world.

"My father was a fan of Miles, and our surname is Davis, so it was an easy choice for him."

"And you happen to play the trumpet, too. That's amazing."

Harry did not have a middle name. He added the "Miles" as a gimmick because he was a fan of Miles Davis and thought this would be very cool.

"Let's say my father pushed me to choose the trumpet, but after the first time I had one in my hands, I knew this was the instrument I wanted to play."

"That's alright then, Mister Harry Miles Davis. You will be starting next Monday. As per the schedule, you will be teaching three hours every day and on Thursdays you will rehearse with the band."

"I can't wait to meet the band members. I'm eager to see where I can take this group."

"Don't thank me, young man. Just teach the kids some music, will you?

A handshake between the two men signified the start of Harry's teaching career in London.

Harry's dream had always been making a living out of

music. Playing the trumpet for a famous band, recording albums, and touring the world, were his plan since he could ever remember, but that had never happened. His biggest achievement to date was performing three nights in a row at the *Blues Basement* in Luton in front of seventy people.

The next best thing was teaching music, and after many attempts at it, he finally got the job at Rosswell Grammar, a middle-class private school with over a thousand students. When he left the school that afternoon, he felt the satisfaction of finally making his musical knowledge help pay his bills.

London, 1977

"There will be a skinny crowd tonight. Fucking rain."

Harry looked at Marge as she spoke. She was still the beautiful and hyperactive girl he met nine years earlier who admired his trumpet playing and was always looking for a new gig for them.

"Crowds in here are always thin. The popular clubs have punk rockers, like those clowns the Ramones," said Rory while tuning his bass.

Paul, the drummer, was quiet as usual, and rarely engaged in chit chat with the others. He was there to do a job and go home.

"To be honest, I don't care too much about empty rooms. The few patrons who come here really appreciate jazz, and I enjoy playing for them," replied Harry.

"Some of them don't give a crap, man. Look at those kids."

Rory pointed to a group of youngsters seating by the jukebox. Some had spiky hair, others a mohawk hairdo and others had completely shaven their heads. Orange and purple were their preferred hair colours, as well as dog collars and black leather outfits.

"Imagine if we were nineteen years old today. Would we be dressed like them?" asked Rory.

"Mate, we're black. I've never seen a black punk

rocker. I think we would be wearing massive afros, bell bottom jeans and a collection of gold chains instead."

Marge and Rory laughed. Paul smiled.

As they started the second set of the night, Harry noticed a middle-aged black man at the bar, drinking a pint. He was bald and looked familiar.

The band breezed through the set. The punk kids were loud and did not care about the music, but the rest of the patrons were appreciative of the performance. Even though the place was half empty, the applause they received after each song managed to silence the loud kids. The bald man uttered a few enthusiastic bravos after they played *Round Midnight* and lifted his glass to the band.

Once the set ended, Harry went to the bar to order beers for the band.

"You guys are really good," said a white man with greying hair who was drinking at the bar.

"That's very nice of you, brother."

"Well, to be totally honest, you're really good. The other two are just decent musicians."

"That's not very nice, sir," Harry's tone of voice changed in a second. He was very protective of his fellow band members.

"Sorry, mate, but that's how it is. I'm not saying they're bad, but they're not at your level."

"And who are you to make such comments, a record producer or something?"

"Yep, you got that right. Joe Fitzgerald from Cerberus Records," the man extended his hand to Harry.

"Cerberus? As in the label that Dexter Brown plays for?"

"That's right, mate."

"And what are you doing in this run-down pub? This is too far away from Piccadilly."

"A good question, my friend. The rain got me on my way to the subway and this place offered shelter, beer and jazz music."

"Well, I'm glad you enjoyed our music tonight."

Harry grabbed the tray with four pints of ale, ready to go back to his group.

"Are you playing again tomorrow?" said Joe.

"Yes man, we are. It's our last night in this place."

"One last question, do you guys have a name?"

Harry thought about it for a few seconds.

"Yes, we do. We are the Sultans. The Sultans of Swing."

"Harry, you're only thirty-five, I don't know why you insist on using these stupid suspenders. They make you look old," said Marge from the bed as Harry was getting dressed.

"They are part of my image. People are used to seeing me in these."

"Yeah, right. Surely the punk kids are sitting at the club anxious to see the black trumpeter in his suspenders tonight. Make sure you bring a pen for the autographs."

Harry laughed. He loved Marge's wit.

"Have you thought about what the band will do next? We haven't got anything lined up for the next couple of months. Jazz clubs are closing or moving away from jazz music."

Harry looked at Marge through the mirror while fixing his tie.

"Maybe my performing career is over. My days of busking at train stations and playing for fifty pounds a night in basements are behind me. I don't have any regrets. I gave everything I had everywhere I played, and for the first time I have decent day job."

Marge stood up and embraced Harry from behind, kissing him on the neck.

"Yeah, if you tell yourself that a few more times, you'll end up believing it."

Harry laughed again, but this time Marge wasn't right.

When they arrived at the club, the place was almost

full. It was a warm and dry Saturday night, and the bar was packed with people taking advantage of the happy hour.

"Are we ready, Harry?" asked Rory, always pumped up before the first set, probably because of some chemical help.

"All good, Rory. Paul, you ready?"

"Always, boss. Let's go."

Without any introduction, Paul started rattling his snare drum, Rory thumped the strings of his bass, and they were off to the first set.

Harry's trumpet sounded like carnival, and the band played a series of jazz standards like *Take Five* and *Autumn Leaves*. Every solo was original, and the bass and drums were as coordinated as they had ever been. Harry remembered that evening years ago when he met Marge. Today the music sounded as perfect as it did back then.

During the break, Harry spotted the bald black man in the bar again, and he was chatting with Joe, the producer.

Many patrons came to their table to say how much they liked the music. The most surprising was a tall kid with green spiky hair and piercings everywhere who was wearing black leather pants with suspenders.

"You guys are great," said the kid. "I'm not into trumpet playing bands, but what you did up there? Just wow. That was fucking cool."

"Well, the trumpeter with the suspenders has been validated by a punk rocker in suspenders. Talk about an irony," said Marge.

At the end of the final set, people cheered the band like Harry had never seen. It was as if they knew this was the last performance of his underground career.

"Thanks for your support, guys. We are the Sultans of Swing."

Harry and the boys stepped down from the stage. Rory and Paul were excited about their recent success, but Harry just fell a sense of modest achievement. He had not told the others his intentions of calling it quits. He would eventually do so.

When he put the trumpet into its case, he felt sadness, like he was closing the coffin of a loved one, but he knew he didn't have anything else to offer as a performer. He had reached as high as he could.

When he approached the bar to order a drink, Joe came up to him. He had two beers, one for Harry and another one for Marge.

"Harry, tonight's performance was better than yesterday's. And let me tell you, you played some of the best trumpet solos I've heard in years."

"Thanks Joe. It means a lot coming from you. I'll drink to that."

"By the way, Harry Davis, I'm not here for a second night in a row for no reason. After listening to you twice, I'd like to offer The Sultans a contract with Cerberus. What do you think?"

Harry was stunned. Minutes ago, he had finished what

he thought was his last performance, and now this guy was offering them a contract.

"Wow. I'm more than flattered, but I have a question. How did you know my name was Harry Davis? I don't recall telling you that."

"Your father over there. He was very proud of you tonight. He told me he never got around to seeing you perform live until last night. I think you should go over and have a chat to him. I believe there is a lot you need to catch up on."

That night, Joe Fitzgerald went home with a sense of achievement, but he wasn't sure if it was due to the signing of a phenomenal trumpeter, or because he got caught in the middle of a long-awaited father and son reunion.